Moments in Time

When One Heart Opens,

Two Hearts Collide

NINA C. PAYNE

This book is dedicated to the loving memory of my brother and best friend, Charlie, and my adoring father.

"Do not fear death…only the unlived life.
You don't have to live forever, you just have to live"

Natalie Babbitt

Acknowledgements

First and foremost I would like to acknowledge my husband, Walter. Your, love, support and encouragement is what made this book possible. My children, my two major blessings, Cameron and Christian, for your endless patience and understanding with my long days and nights at the computer and for being my greatest cheerleaders. To my brilliant brother Wade, whose first words when hearing part of the book said, "Yeah, I hear you but I don't feel you". You made me dig deep and tap into a place of vulnerability and fear. You gave new life to my story. Howard Richmond MD, you have been a constant and consistent force in my life. Your friendship is invaluable to me and your input and feedback in the process of writing this book, priceless. Michael Fukumura, my mentor and teacher—your insights, profound humility and guidance will forever be etched in my heart, my mind and my soul. You embody yoga, strength and courage. To Mike Stephens, for helping me through a time I never thought I could get through. Finally, to my Mom, all my family, my friends and my "yoga crew", you all know who you are. Thank you from the bottom of my heart.

Namaste

Prologue

I've been practicing yoga for years. I even became a yoga teacher. Hot yoga—really hot yoga—is my preference. I recently started practicing at a new studio closer to my children's school. Same hot yoga, same style—you know, the one with the guy who wears a Speedo and sits on this giant podium that looks like a throne in the front of the studio. I've never taken a class from him, but I heard he barks orders and hurls insults at his faithful followers and unsuspecting newbies. Anyway, the yoga is great, and this guy's managed to build a multibillion-dollar organization with yoga, the supposed antithesis of materialism and money. So kudos to the man for that alone. I really like this new studio. Not too big, cozy, and the few teachers I've taken classes with have been really good.

On this day I walk in and notice a different teacher. His back is to me. I know I haven't taken class with him yet because I've only had female teachers. As he turns and faces me, our eyes lock instantaneously. My breath is momentarily taken away, and we are staring at each other. He also seems to be taken aback a bit.

After what feels like an eternity, he composes himself and says confidently, "Hi, I'm Daniel. Don't think I've seen you here before."

I'm not quite as composed or nearly as confident as I begin to sign in. I clumsily respond, "I'm new—well not new as in new, like new to yoga, just new here." What's wrong with me?

He looks at the sign-in sheet and says, "Cassandra Peyton."

I quietly reply, "Yes."

"Nice to meet you, Cassandra. Have a great class."

As I go to place my mat down, I wonder what just happened. Did he feel that too? And if he did, what was that? Never, even in fifteen years of marriage, have I ever felt that kind of exchange with anyone, least of all someone I just met. Sure, I notice obviously attractive men. I am human, after all, married, not dead. This—this was different. This stirred something inside me. I keep trying to convince myself it was nothing, but it definitely wasn't nothing. Nothing doesn't usually have a way of making you feel something. *Let it go*, I think to myself. *It was just a momentary lapse of whatever. Focus, just focus.*

Mat down, I inspect myself in the mirror. I have long, thick, naturally curly, dark brown hair. At five foot six, I'm lean, strong, and flexible. I have olive skin and brown eyes. My best friend, Mark, and my husband, Steve, say I have an exotic and mysterious aura about me. I pretty much keep to myself, friendly and somewhat aloof, which some read as arrogant. Truth be told, I may come off as confident, but even the drive to the yoga studio is excruciating for me. I feel anxious and insecure. I'm probably one of the few people who feel like they need Xanax on their way to yoga. Most days I have to talk myself into going.

The conversation goes something like this: *OK, just get into your yoga clothes. You don't have to go; just get dressed…Now get your gear together, water, yoga towel, mat. Great!…Get into the car, and just drive in that direction. Remember, Cass, you don't have to go…Park the car, and now go in and place your mat down. You could always leave, saying you had some family emergency. Just go in.* So it goes. Once I'm in the studio, I know even before putting my mat down I'm staying. After the first breathing exercise, it's like I'm in my own world, without any worries or concerns.

Identifying why I have this internal struggle getting to yoga is a whole other animal because I'm not exactly sure why. Yoga is like an exposé, a mirror on my life. On my mat I practice with so much control and discipline, never really letting my defenses down. Off the mat, it's pretty much the same. I'm very structured and disciplined there as well. I rarely let my guard down except maybe to my husband, my brother Andy, my best friend, Mark, my sweet dad, and my kids. I couldn't even begin to describe what reckless abandon feels like, on or off the mat.

Class begins, and Daniel steps up to the podium. He's wearing what looks like bike shorts. His shirt is off now. I would guess him to be in his early forties. He's about five foot eleven, has thick, light brown, wavy hair with visible signs of gray and hazel eyes. His hair is just past his shoulders, and he wears it pulled back into a ponytail. He's lean, tan, with well-defined muscles. *Man he looks good,* I think while my stomach does this weird flip thing. *Focus, Cassandra. Just focus,* I remind myself again. I know in yoga we're supposed to check our egos at the door, but not this day, not in this class, not with this teacher.

We start with a breathing exercise. I calm down and start to get into a zone. The zone for me is where I can tune out everything around me and be completely immersed in the moment.

"Breathe in that cosmic life force, energy, prana, all around you. Fill your lungs. Expand your lungs. Exhale, big 'ha' sound. Exhale it all out. Keep exhaling. Keep exhaling, getting ready for that next inhale. Inhale deep into your lungs. Breathe into the back of your throat, elbows high, spine straight. Now exhale all the air out. Sounding strong today, everyone. Nice!" he says happily.

When we come out of our first forward bend of the series, he exclaims, "Welcome to your life everyone! Are you feeling it?"

The class chimes back, "Feeling it!"

I'm grinning. I'm not used to a teacher in this style of yoga being so interactive with the class. He's charming and filled with so much joy for teaching. After the initial series of warm-up postures, I've a good sweat going. I love the way my muscles glisten through the beads of sweat pouring down every inch of my body. I never feel happier, calmer, sexier than when I'm on my mat.

I pull off an amazingly powerful class, balanced, poised, and strong. Proud of myself, I walk out and, feigning modesty, thank Daniel for class. He pauses and stares at me. There's that look again! I can't help but stare right back into his eyes. There's no mistaking the attraction I feel toward him.

Finally he says, "You have a beautiful practice, Cassandra. Hope to see you again soon, and welcome."

I smile and say, "Thanks, Daniel." I find myself loving the sound of his voice and the way he says my name. With that I leave, get into my car, and just sit for a while in a state of joyful bliss that only this yoga can give me. Ninety minutes of heaven, ninety minutes of hell.

⁓

When I get home, I go straight to my computer and go to the studio's website. I've been there before but only to get the address and to quickly check the class schedule. I open their home page, and there it is: "Directors, Daniel and Cheryl Evans," with a picture of them both. I read Daniel's bio and quickly realize he's in his early fifties. *Wow*, I think, *yoga really is the fountain of youth!* I'm in my early forties and have been told I could easily pass for my thirties, so maybe there's some truth to that. So he's not just a teacher; he's the studio owner.

I click to the class schedule, hoping to see who teaches and when. Nothing. Just the days and times. *Damn*, I think, *it sure would be nice to know when he teaches.* The thought of experiencing what I felt today and having my stomach do that weird flip thing, like I'm some kind of schoolgirl having her first crush, scares me. On the other hand, I'm filled with excitement and anticipation at the prospect of seeing him again. The rational part of me knows this isn't something I should be entertaining. The other part, apparently more powerful, can't stop thinking about him. I'm married. He's married. End of story. I look at his picture again. There's something about him I can't seem to shake.

I walk away from my computer and head to the bathroom to shower. I wonder what about him caused such a reaction within me. My husband, Steve, is wonderful—a great provider, loving father. The sex between us has always been—even after two kids—regular, though somewhat routine. Sure we've had our moments and ups and downs, but for the most part, we've an incredible life.

Steve's company is solid. He built it from the ground up. He's a private investor, like Bernie Madoff, only legal. He's a workaholic by most people's standards, mine included. When he walks through the door at the end of the day, he quickly kisses me and the kids, asks about everyone's day, and then announces that he has a "couple" of phone calls to make and has to put a "few" deals together.

"Just call me when dinner is ready, Cass. I'm really buried this week," he always says hurriedly as he makes his way upstairs to his office.

This week? I laugh to myself. *Try maybe this month, this year, this life.* Whenever I bring up to him that he's working way too much and the kids and I'd love to have more quality time with him, he responds with, "I'm doing the best I can, Cass. Do you know how big our nut is? I mean, look around you. Our kids' school alone is fifty thousand a year…" I immediately feel guilty and tell him I understand.

〜〜

I get out of my wet clothes and into the shower. Now that the kids are older and in school, gone are the days of speed eating, speed showering, speed brushing and grooming. Doing all of these things plus trying to get the kids ready, the house picked up, and myself out the door successfully felt like an Olympic event instead of simple, everyday tasks. I thoroughly enjoy having the luxury of a warm, almost hot shower.

I tilt my head back to wet my already damp hair and love the feel of the warm water streaming down my body. Life seems to be moving slowly. As I shampoo my hair, the smell of lavender, one of my favorite scents, begins to permeate the air. I rinse my hair and start to wash my body. I bring the lavender soap bar close to my face, close my eyes, and take a long inhale. How I love that smell! I lather my body, starting with my neck, then my shoulders, chest, and breasts. I pause and slowly massage each breast with each hand. I can feel my nipples become erect to my touch. I tilt my head back again as the water flows down my head and shoulders and down the small of my back. I'm moving in a trance-like state, completely engrossed in each sensation. I begin to caress my stomach and move down lower between my thighs. I'm feeling increasingly aroused.

Just then my cell phone rings. I contemplate not answering it and letting it go to voice mail. No, I have to answer. What if it's the kids' school calling to let me know one of them is sick or, worse, is on the way to the emergency room with blood gushing out of his or her head after being severely injured in PE? I rinse off quickly, grab the towel, and see it's my mom.

"Dammit!" I say out loud, frustrated. I calm down and answer. "Hi, Mom."

"Hi, dear," she replies.

"Hey, Mom, can I call you back? I just got out of the shower, and I'm standing here dripping wet," I say hurriedly.

"Oh sure, dear. I just wanted to let you know that your aunt and uncle are coming in from San Francisco two weekends from now. Let's see, that would be the twenty-third. Or is it the twenty-fifth? Let me just check the calendar here…No, it's the twenty-third. Anyway, we're planning dinner for them on that Saturday, so please don't make any plans. I've already spoken to your brothers and sister, and they plan on being here."

Annoyed now more than ever, not only at the interruption but that the "standing-here-dripping-wet part" seems to have flown right over her head, trying to contain may exasperation, I say, "Yeah, Mom, let me check with Steve and make sure we're clear for that weekend, and I'll get back to you."

She continues. "Well, you know, dear"—I hate it when she calls me dear—"we expect you to be here. You know how much we love to have the whole family together."

Calmly and with restraint, although a bit curt, I respond, "Mom, I have to dry off. I'll call you later today after I've had a chance to talk to Steve."

She says, "Oh, I'm sorry, dear." One day I'll tell her to stop calling me dear. "I don't mean to keep you. So how are the kids?"

Oh Jesus, Mary, Mother of Christ! I say in my head. Now really holding back, mustering up the very last of my patience, I say, "Fine, fine. Everyone's fine. Call you later. OK, love you." I quickly hang up, not waiting for a response.

One

I have a very different relationship with my mother than I do with my father. As I was growing up, my mother was emotionally distant and very concerned with keeping up appearances, usually at the expense of how we kids were feeling. Our image always came first. We were taught not to make waves, and we swept so many things under the rug Mount Everest would look like a molehill in comparison. Her face never lit up when I walked into a room; if anything it was a look of annoyance and disappointment. Her way of disciplining me was by guilting and shaming me. She'd also slap and hit sometimes, usually with a slipper.

Besides Andy, I have another brother, the eldest, William, and an older sister, Allison, who is third in line. I'm the youngest. Andy's the favorite—I mean everyone's favorite—but he and I have the strongest bond of all. We have since we were kids. He always seemed to like me and loved having me around. He included me whenever he could and even taught me how to ride a bike. That's one moment I'll never forget. I kept wobbling and falling, and he kept making me get up and try again.

"I don't care if we're here all day and night; you'll ride this bike today!" he said to me enthusiastically. "You can do this,

Cass. I know you can." (When I was a kid, he and my dad were the only two who called me Cass. I didn't like it when anyone else did, and if they tried, I'd politely say, "Cassandra." I still do, in fact.)

Right around sunset, after quite a few spills off that bike and plenty of scrapes and bruises, Andy was holding onto the back of the bike, and without my knowledge he let go. I went quite a ways before I heard him yelling from a distance, "You got it, Cass. You're riding a bike. You're doing it!" I looked back and began to wobble as he yelled, with both of his arms stretched straight up toward the sky, "Don't look back! Just ride, Cass. Ride!" So I did, with a huge smile, the smell of orange blossoms in the air and the warm summer wind blowing on my face. What an amazing feeling! Andy was proud of me, and that was the greatest feeling of all. We're not just brother and sister; we're best friends.

William kind of broke off from the family right after high school, never being one to deal with a false sense of propriety. I guess he rebelled in a way: put himself through college and became a very successful entrepreneur. He married young, a beautiful Asian woman he met while in college. They have three amazing kids, two boys and a girl. They're so witty, kind, and intelligent. He did good!

Allison and I aren't very close, and I can tell she's a bit jealous of my relationship with Andy, wanting what he and I share. Allison went off, also marrying someone she met in college. She has three kids as well. I'm not as close to her and her husband as I am to William and his family. In fact, I don't care for her husband, Kyle. Steve and I just tolerate him for the sake of Allison and the kids. It's not even that we don't like him; we just don't get him. He always speaks like it's from a script, always careful to be politically correct, and tends to ask the most random questions. He and Allison are constantly at my parents' house, and they both have my mom wrapped around their fingers. They know just what to say to her. To anyone listening, it sounds patronizing and condescending, but my mom eats it up.

Andy and I never finished college, each of us for very different reasons. I became an idealistic revolutionary, determined to save the world from itself, and Andy—well, he lacked a clear vision of where he wanted to be or what he wanted to do. He ended up working for my father's insurance company. He does pretty well. Although you'd never look at Andy and think *salesman*, people like him—really like him—so they trust him. There isn't much selling involved. My father retired about ten years ago, and Andy's been running the business successfully ever since. He primarily relies on repeat business and referrals, not doing much marketing and advertising. He's never been out to make a killing; he's too down-to-earth for that. He just likes a simple, peaceful lifestyle.

Andy was married for about ten years. I never understood that relationship or the attraction. None of us liked her; we just tolerated her for Andy's sake. Andy kept putting off having kids with her. I think deep inside he knew the relationship wouldn't last and throwing children in the mix would just complicate things. I know Andy wanted kids, but he now says he is very content being a surrogate father to all his nieces and nephews. There isn't a better uncle than he is. He absolutely lives for the kids, taking them to the movies, golfing, camping, the beach. They adore him in return because they know his love is genuine and he is sincerely interested in who they are.

Andy divorced about three years ago, a really messy divorce—it's good they never had kids. Andy has since reunited with his high school sweetheart, Tracy. They're beautiful together, and she treats him with the love and respect he needs and deserves. Love should never hurt, and Andy finally gets that.

If Andy's everyone's favorite, I'm my dad's favorite. Dad's relationship with William has always been a bit contentious. I guess Dad expected more from William because he's the oldest, and he rode him quite hard. Allison stayed out of Dad's way for the most part. My dad is strong, silent, and very authoritative. He doesn't tolerate talking back or disrespect in any way. I'm his soft spot, and he's mine. I can make him smile even when he's angry or disappointed with me. One time he was wearing these pajamas that had these ridiculous-looking Bermuda-short bottoms. I must've been around fifteen or sixteen. I did something, I can't remember what. He was yelling at me and going on and on. I was looking down, trying hard not to laugh.

He finally screamed, "Look at me when I'm talking to you!" I looked up, and he could clearly see I was smiling and holding back laughter. "What's so funny? Is something funny here?" he yelled even louder. I didn't respond and was holding back laughter. "Answer me, dammit!" Now the neighbors could hear him.

Cautiously I said, knowing this could get worse very quickly, "Dad, it's really hard to take you seriously when you're yelling at me in those Bermuda pajama bottoms." He stared at me with disbelief; I was holding my breath at this point. Finally he cracked a smile and yelled at me to go to my room.

Two

I dry off and get dressed. The usual—T-shirt and jeans. Not "mom" jeans. Stylish, low-rise jeans and a form-fitting T-shirt that accentuates my tight abs and small but firm breasts. I say firm, but I had to have them lifted. No implants, just lifted. They were like down to my knees after nursing both kids. I went from a 34C before kids to 38DD during pregnancy to who-knows-what-those-were after nursing. See, these are things people don't tell you when you start having kids. You won't sleep, you'll be sucked dry, you won't recognize your body, and there will be days when you understand why animals sometimes eat their young. Thankfully I didn't get stretch marks. I practiced yoga during and after both pregnancies, so my abs and body bounced back quickly. I spray a little gel in my hair and let it dry naturally. My makeup is minimal—eyeliner, a little mascara, a touch of lipstick, and I'm good to go.

I go about the daily routine of my life—cleaning, laundry, grocery shopping, running errands, and one of the favorite parts of my day, picking up my kids from school. I have two. My son, Lance—we call him L—is the spitting image of me. Dark, curly hair he likes to wear long, close to his shoulders, and these beautiful chocolate eyes with long eyelashes. Lance is laid-back and

5

easygoing. His passion is quiet but unbridled. He can sit and draw or read for hours. At twelve, he's beyond his years, an old soul of sorts. He loves music; he listens to everything from old Steely Dan to Pink Floyd, from jazz and blues to his favorite, alternative, indie, obscure-type bands. Say Justin Bieber or Miley Cyrus to him three times, and he'll throw up on the spot. Nothing mainstream for him. He's my little anarchist, very inside his head, a critical and analytical thinker.

My daughter, Joey, fourteen, is named after a character in one of my favorite movies, *Guess Who's Coming to Dinner*. Joey is stunning. She has long, thick light brown hair, hazel eyes, porcelain skin, and Angelina Jolie lips. She's a mix of both Steve and me, taking Steve's hair color, green eyes, straight hair, and full lips. From me she gets the thickness of my hair, my high cheekbones, and the shape of my eyes and face. Unlike her brother, she's fiery and passionate about everything. She lives life on her terms and is very black and white in how she sees her world. She can't stand injustice of any kind and is very vocal about it. Joey is witty, sarcastic, and has the best sense of humor, one of the few people who can bring me to tears with laughter. Of course at fourteen, she's discovering boys, her sexuality, and the power it holds.

I always try to stay one step ahead of them, but that's not always easy. I've found I have to constantly be listening and paying attention more to what they aren't telling me and find creative ways to allow them to open up in a way that feels safe to them. I'd like to think that so far I have both their ears, but I guess most parents feel like that.

Fortunately for Steve and me, our kids are compassionate and truly care about others and how they feel. Of course, they're still kids, a tween and a teen, and can test our patience with the best of them, but I run a tight ship and leave very little room for bad behavior. I always tell my kids, "I don't care what you're going through; there's never an excuse for bad behavior. Never!" Steve, on the other hand, leaves the disciplining to me. He's laid-back with his parenting style—I'm not even sure he has one. The kids know they can push the boundaries a lot further with Steve than with me.

On my way to pick up the kids, I call Mark and tell him about what happened in class. Mark and I have been best friends for several years. We met at a yoga teacher's training. Mark quite literally looks like an Adonis, a Greek god, tall, tan, statuesque, muscular, salt-and-pepper hair, blue eyes – a visual delight. The only thing more beautiful than he is his yoga practice. I talked a lot about him at home during training. Steve asked once, "You two don't have something going on, do you?"

To which I replied, "You two would be more likely to have something going on than he and I." He quickly got the picture.

Neither Mark nor I do much teaching these days. We both did right after training and for about a couple of years afterward. Occasionally we'll sub for someone, and maybe someday we'll teach again, but for now our lives are full and busy. He's a successful freelance photographer. He took some beautiful nude yoga stills of me in various postures, had them framed, and gave them to me for my birthday last year. They're done very tastefully and are hanging upstairs in my yoga room.

"Hey, Mark, how's it going?" I ask.

"Hey, Cass, pretty good, just working. My latest project, photographing buildings downtown. I can't think of anything more mundane and less interesting. But it pays the bills, so I shouldn't complain. What are you up to?"

"Going to pick up Joey and Lance. Mark, something happened today in class. There was this teacher, Daniel. I felt this jolt, like nothing I have ever felt before. It was immediate and intense."

"What do you mean? Like an attraction?" he asks.

"Yes, exactly. An attraction, a very powerful attraction," I respond.

"Well, now that is interesting and not mundane. Thanks for breaking up the monotony of my day. Cass, don't get yourself all freaked out, these things happen—not to you though. Maybe you should be concerned. Or at least cautious," he says, trying to offer support. "So, what was it about him?" he asks.

"I'm not even sure. I mean, he's attractive, but I run into attractive men every day. This was different; I can't even put words to it. Something in his eyes, I think, I guess—I don't know," I say, sounding confused.

"Just see what happens next time you see him. Maybe it was just like this one-time thing. You know, lust at first sight. Those things tend to taper off as quickly as they begin. I wouldn't worry about it," he says.

"OK, Mark. I'm just pulling up to the school. I'll talk to you later."

"OK, sweetie. Give my angels a kiss from me."

"I will. Bye."

＿＿＿

I pull into the school. They go to a small private school in Del Mar by the coast, close to where we live. They love it. Steve and I love it. The kids are taught to self-advocate and rely less on their parents. The parent-teacher conferences are student led. If homework isn't complete for whatever reason, it's up to the student to do the explaining, not the parent. That teaches them accountability and doesn't leave any room for the parents to bail them out, so to speak.

I arrive at the school. I text the kids that I'm there. They come out separately and get into the car. They're both on their iPhones. Lance tells me, "I have a song I want to play for you."

Joey says, "So do I, next."

Lance plays me a song from Green Day. "You have to listen to the lyrics Mom, really listen. I'm not responsible for the language, just to warn you." He knows I don't mind nudity or language when it's not gratuitous and adds to the artistic expression of whatever medium is being used.

Joey next plays me a song called "Skinny Love" by Birdy. They know how much I love music. The music they listen to really gives me a glimpse into their minds—Lance a rebel against convention and Joey a hopeless romantic. I rarely, if ever, turn on the TV, but I always have music playing. Lance plays the guitar and drums, Joey the piano. TV, these days, is just shit in my opinion. I can't even go to the movies. Steve loves to go and begs me to go with him. A movie theater is something akin to Chinese water torture for me. Trapped in a room full of people who are making all kinds of noises, chomping on popcorn, talking loudly, and don't get me started on if someone sneezes or coughs! I'll never forget that scene from the movie *Outbreak* where that really sick guy sneezes, and in slow motion they show all the droplets of mucus and spit being transported throughout the theater. It's not a pleasant experience for me, so I just don't go anymore. Steve goes with friends or takes the kids; lucky for him they're older now so they can see something they will all enjoy.

"So how was your day?" Lance asks. He never forgets to ask about my day.

"The usual, and, of course, yoga this morning," I reply.

"How was it?" they both ask right about the same time.

"Hot!" I exclaim. They both laugh, and I laugh right along with them, more at the subtle hidden meaning that only I know.

Three

The next morning I walk into yoga class hoping Daniel is teaching. To my disappointment he isn't. *Oh well*, I think, *probably best*. I place my mat down and start warming up. While doing a forward bend, I notice a mat being placed close to mine. I don't look up, keeping to myself, when I hear a familiar voice say, "Hi, Cassandra. Mind if I practice next to you?" My stomach starts doing flip-flops. I don't know why it never occurred to me that of course he practices here as well!

I manage to say, "Hi, Daniel. Yes—I mean no, no I don't mind." He remembered my name. That's interesting and flattering, but he's the studio owner, I rationalize, so he probably makes it his job to remember names, making his students feel special so they keep coming back.

"How are you?" he asks with this grin on his face I can't really read.

"I'm fine, you?" I respond.

He pauses, looking at me with that same look as yesterday and still grinning.

"Fine, really fine," he says, kind of shaking his head from side to side, smiling as he finishes getting set up for class.

The lights turn on, a sign class is starting and everyone should stand. He leans over toward me and whispers, "Have a great class, Cassandra." I already love it when he says my name.

"You, too," I whisper back, smiling.

Practicing next to him is amazing. He's so strong, his postures beautiful. I'm loving keeping up. I hold the postures and purposely move in and out of them in unison with him. We're moving together, both very focused and determined, completely in sync. We never look at each other, but it's as if there's this synergy flowing between us, and I'm curious if he feels it as well. Our bodies are drenched in sweat. I hear the sound of sweat dripping onto our mats when we hold a pose.

When class is over and right before Savasana, our final resting pose, Daniel leans in toward me, wiping his face, and playfully asks, "Was that as good for you as it was for me?"

I smile shyly and lie down. Although I can't understand it, this attraction is real, really real. I wonder if it's mutual, but I don't know him well enough and think maybe he's like this with all his students. I come out of Savasana before he does and start gathering my things. Almost everyone has left. He gets up and says quietly, "Cassandra, are you coming tomorrow morning?"

"Yes," I reply. "Are you practicing or teaching?"

"Teaching," he answers.

"I'll see you tomorrow then," I say, smiling, and walk away.

⌒

I'm eager for class the next day, especially knowing Daniel will be teaching. The traffic from my kids' school to the studio is unusually busy, and I start to wonder if I'm even going to make it. It's literally bumper to bumper. It has to be an accident; it's never like this. "Come on, come on," I keep saying out loud. It's not good yoga etiquette to walk into class late; it disrupts the flow of the class and can be distracting for the students. I can't remember the last time I was late to a class. I'm always early, one of the first to arrive.

Up ahead I can see there's an accident being cleared. The traffic is moving faster, but I still don't think I'll make it on time. And I won't walk in late. I pull up to the studio about two minutes before class is scheduled to begin.

I quickly make my way into the studio, and Daniel joyfully exclaims, "There she is! Hi, Cassandra. Didn't think you were going to make it."

I can't help but smile and reply, "Hi, Daniel. Got stuck in traffic."

I sign in, walk into the yoga room, and quickly set up my mat. Lights go on. We all stand. Class begins. This is only my second class with Daniel, but I can already tell he's an incredible teacher. His instruction is precise and so relevant to the pose. Many teachers in this particular style of yoga sound like they're reciting a dialogue. Daniel is the dialogue. He infuses himself into every word and makes it his own. Each instruction is filled with the subtle nuances of the posture we're doing. You have to listen carefully in this type of yoga; the teachers rarely demonstrate the postures. The positive aspect of this way of teaching is the students learn to find and feel their own way into the posture.

"Yoga can transform you, from the inside out, with daily, consistent practice. You'll be, better, stronger, healthier, happier," Daniel states between postures. "Accept and transcend as you mindfully move in and out of the postures."

That really resonates with me, "accept and transcend." As we practice acceptance and completely surrender to it, we can begin to transform our bodies and our minds. Eventually we can go even beyond that and transcend to a higher level of consciousness and awareness on and off the mat. *Accept and transcend,* I think again, really taking that in as I practice each posture.

He reminds us to smile, breathe, and relax. "Take a break whenever you feel you need to; without judgment, without attachment. Feel how good it feels to be on your mat, breathing, moving, stretching. Feel how good it feels to come alive with your breath as your guide." he says as I grin. Although he commands the room and is authoritative, there's a lightness to his teaching, a joy, and it's contagious.

⌒

For the next six months or so, I know his teaching schedule and when he practices. He never fails to remind me anyway. Our relationship—for lack of a better word because it certainly isn't a friendship—has reached a point where we exchange flirtatious glances and tease each other. The attraction is mutual, and from what I can tell, he isn't at all like this with the other female students in class. In fact, he seems reserved and almost impersonal. One day after class he tells me a few of the regulars and teachers are going to go down the street for smoothies and asks if I'd like to come.

I say, "I'd like to, but I didn't bring a change of clothes." There is no way I am going anywhere with him like this, all sweaty and wet. "Besides, I am meeting my brother Andy for lunch. I'd love to bring him with me to class one day. You would really like him, one of the nicest people you'll ever meet."

"OK," he says, sounding disappointed. "Next time then, and I'd love to meet your brother." As I start to walk out, he comes up from behind and says discreetly, "Bring a change of clothes on Friday."

"OK, I will."

He smiles happily and says, "Nice."

⌒

As I walk to my car, I can't help but think about Daniel's wife, Cheryl. I've taken quite a few classes with her, and we've had several short conversations through the months. People really don't get much kinder than she is; when she smiles, the room lights up. I think she's a bit older than Daniel, maybe in her late fifties. She has light brown hair, which she wears in a bob right above her chin. Her sweetness makes this thing with Daniel even more awkward. Nothing's ever happened and nothing ever will, but just talking to and somewhat knowing the woman whose husband you have this enormous attraction for can feel uncomfortable.

⁓

*A*ndy cancelled lunch. That night I call him for our usual nightly chat. He hasn't been feeling well. His back and shoulder have really been bothering him for the past three or so months. The doctor said it's sciatica and he probably pulled something in his shoulder from golf. Poor guy has been in and out of physical therapy and living on pain pills and even losing a lot of weight. I finally persuaded him to go back to his doctor and insist on an x-ray or something. This is no way to live, and if anything, it's getting worse. He's been taking increasingly more time off of work to the point my dad has had to step back in and help out. He did go back, and the doctor ordered a CAT scan, PET scan, bone scan, and some blood work. Andy is waiting for the results. I wonder why it took so long for them to do something, and when they finally do why they order every test under the sun.

"Hey, Andy, how are you feeling today? Any results back yet?" I ask.

"Yeah," he says. "All of them."

"Well, what is it? What did the doctor say? Slipped disc? Frozen shoulder? What?" He's quiet. "Andy, what is it?" I ask again, concerned.

"I don't know, Cass. His nurse said the doctor wants me to come in Friday morning to give me the results. She wouldn't say anything else." He sounds worried.

"Andy, I wouldn't read too much into that. That's how they do things. I mean, obviously, something is going on—you're in so much pain—but I'm sure it's nothing too serious. He probably just wants to talk over different treatment options, like maybe surgery if the disc is really messed up. You know, that kind of stuff," I try to reassure him.

"Yeah, you're probably right," he replies, not sounding very convinced.

"Hey, I'll drive you. We'll go together, OK?"

"I'd like that, Cass."

"Of course, Andy. Listen, try to get some rest, and I'll see you Friday morning. What time is your appointment?" I ask.

"We have to be there at ten fifteen," he replies.

"I'll pick you up at nine fifteen in case we run into traffic."

"Sounds good," he says. "Thanks."

"No problem. Talk to you tomorrow. Love you, Andy."

"Love you, too, Cass."

Well there goes yoga and smoothies on Friday, I think, laughing. Oh well, I'm not too concerned about Andy's tests. It's all routine as far as I'm concerned.

⟋⟋

On the morning of Andy's appointment, I pick him up, and he's in even worse pain than a week and half ago when I last saw him. He brings a pillow in the car and puts it on the seat to support his lower back.

"Geez, Andy, you look awful—pale and even a bit gaunt!" I say, surprised.

"Thanks, Cass. Nice to see you, too," he says sarcastically.

I start driving. Now I'm concerned. Every time I hit a bump in the road, he grimaces and moans. "Sorry, Andy," I keep saying. "We're almost there."

"It's OK. Just easy on those bumps," he says.

"OK, Andy. Don't worry. We'll get you fixed up, even if you need surgery. Hey, it's better than being in all this pain, right?" I say, patting his leg.

"Right, right," he says, grimacing again. We pull up at the doctor's office at ten o'clock. He has a hard time getting out of the car and walking. Andy brings the pillow in and places it on the seat in the reception area, just like in the car. He has his hand on his forehead, rubbing it, clearly in so much pain.

By ten forty, I'm getting really agitated that we've been kept waiting so long. I walk up to the receptionist and ask her when she thinks we'll be seen. She says, "Any minute. The doctor is running a bit late."

Like my kids say, "Thank you, Captain Obvious!" At eleven, I'm past upset. I'm pissed. Andy's in an excruciating amount of pain, and there are three women behind the receptionist area acting like they're on a coffee break.

I walk up to the receptionist again and say quietly but firmly, "Excuse me. This can play out in one of two ways. You either get my brother in right now, like right now, or you pick up that phone and call nine-one-one and get him to the emergency room. See him sitting over there?" I point to him. "That's not happiness on his face; that's extreme pain. So, which is it going to be?"

She gives me a dirty look and gets up from her chair—nice to see it's not permanently affixed to her ass—and walks to the back area of the office.

Lo and behold, a nurse comes to the door and says, "Andrew Stevens?" like we just got there or something. I help Andy up. He has to wait for a moment before he can start walking. The nurse begins walking him to the scale, and I tell her, "No. No weighing in. We just want to see the doctor." Andy can barely tolerate the pain standing up. She begins to say something about the chart. I tell her, "Write 'thin, very thin, thinner than last time,' but he's not getting weighed in." I'm not winning any popularity contests with this doctor's staff, that's for sure.

She puts us into one of the rooms and tells Andy to jump up onto to exam table. Jump, really? Great choice of words. I tell Andy to sit in the chair; I put his pillow the way he likes it, and he sits down. Like in the waiting room, he's rubbing his forehead. What the hell happened? This has been going on awhile, but even in just the last ten days he's so much worse. I tell the nurse, or whatever she is, that we don't want to be kept waiting any longer. She tells me she'll inform the doctor.

Dr. Braunstein comes in about five minutes later with Andy's chart and what looks like big envelopes that must have the films of all those tests he took. He doesn't even apologize for the wait. He shakes Andy's hand and introduces himself to me.

"Are you his significant other?" he says, trying to sound clever.

"Yes," I reply, "very significant. I'm his sister, Cassandra."

He sits on a bench-like chair that's attached to a little desk and opens the chart. "Andy," he begins, "I wish I had better news for you, but we got the results back from all your tests, and the CAT scan showed a lump in your left lung and some mets on the bones in your pelvis and shoulder. The PET scan lit up extensively in those areas. There's also pleural effusion, fluid in your lung, that we'd like to get a sample from for further analysis. The bone scan confirmed that the pelvis, low back area, and shoulder have tumors. That's why you're having so much pain in those areas."

Neither Andy nor I can say anything. I'm just thinking, *This idiot is in the wrong room, talking to the wrong people, looking at the wrong chart.* I'm beyond stunned.

He continues, "Andy, this is very serious, incurable, terminal. We can treat some of the symptoms, radiation will help with the pain in your shoulder and back, and we can start chemo to offer you more time. I want you to meet with Dr. Petal. He's a very good oncologist, and he'll refer you to someone for radiation."

What language is this guy speaking? I just can't take in what he's saying. I feel like I'm in a Charlie Brown cartoon where the parents talk and all you hear is, "Wah, wah, wah!"

I finally say, "What in God's name are you talking about?" I turn to Andy. "Did he say terminal?" Looking back at the doctor, I say, confused, "You throw out words like terminal, and I think airport. You say mets, and I think New York. For the past four months, you have been telling him it's sciatica and a pulled muscle in his shoulder."

Ignoring me, Andy quietly asks, "How much time do I have?"

What? How much time? What's Andy talking about? My head is spinning, and I'm starting to feel sick to my stomach. Dr. Braunstein responds very casually. "Looking at the statistics, about four, maybe six months. We believe we'll find cancer cells in the fluid in your lungs, which makes the prognosis even worse."

Oh my God, he just said cancer! I must be a complete idiot, because that didn't even occur to me till he just said it. "What cancer?" I ask, looking at the doctor, baffled.

"Your brother has lung cancer that has metastasized to his bones. It's advanced, stage four."

I raise my voice to almost shouting. "Well, take it out. Go in and take it out. Nuke it. Do whatever it is you guys do. Just get it out!"

He tries to sound compassionate but blows it by saying, "Alexandra—"

I immediately correct him with clear frustration. "Cassandra!"

"I'm sorry. Cassandra, this is inoperable. There's no cure."

Now I explode. "You pompous, arrogant shell of a man. First you keep us waiting for over forty-five minutes knowing what you're going to tell us, then you sit there reclined with your hands behind your head using terms like terminal, inoperable mastastawhatever like you're giving us yesterday's news. This person sitting right here"—I point to Andy—"the one with all the color drained from his face, the one you just scared the living daylights out of with your death sentence, is someone's son, someone's brother, someone's uncle, someone's lover, and my best friend. I may accept your diagnosis, but I reject your prognosis. Unless you're some kind of seer of the future, you can't possibly know how long he has to live. No possible way!"

He gives another half-assed attempt at compassion and says condescendingly, "I know how difficult this must be for you, and I think it would be good for you both to meet with our palliative care team."

Palliative—now that's a term I do know. That's code for, "We're going to pump you up with so many different kinds of pain meds and sedatives that you'll still be dying, you just won't give a shit."

"No thanks!" I respond defiantly. "Come on, Andy. Let's go; we have work to do."

⟶

We slowly make our way back to the car, and Andy takes a couple of pain pills. Andy looks completely distraught and as if he is fighting back tears. Well, he looks like any man would look after he's just been told he's dying. "Hey, Andy, don't listen to that guy. Forget him. We're going to find you the best care out there. We're going to find a doctor that's going to treat *you* the person, not some statistic. You're going to beat this, Andy. That's your only alternative. Starting today, like right now, you're going to clean up that horrible diet of yours. You eat nothing that has a mother, nothing processed, no sugar, only whole foods and juicing. Green juices till you puke. I'll cook and juice for you every day if I have to. Once we get you out of all this pain, we'll start walking and doing yoga together, no excuses. Every day."

Andy's very quiet and says, "I'm dying."

I pull the car over and tell him to look at me. He continues to stare straight ahead. Very sternly I raise my voice, "Look at me!" Finally he does. "Yes, you're dying. Yes, this is terminal. We're all dying. From the second we're born, we're all one breath closer to death. Life is terminal, Andy. None of us are getting out alive. Death is one of the few things in life we can count on. So, you have a decision to make. We all do. While we're here, what kind of life are we going to choose to live? We live and we die, and everything in between is just our point of view. You can wallow in self-pity or you can get busy living and finding ways to make the best of this really awful situation." I go on, less firm, more sympathetically. "I, for one, refuse to imagine a world without you in it."

With that a flood of tears starts pouring down his face, something I'm not at all used to seeing from him. That sets me off, and now I'm crying right along with him. We hold each other so tight and for so long, no words, just the sound of our hearts breaking into a million pieces.

Four

As we drive, the mood is somber, and we're both silent. A million thoughts run through my head. First things first—we have to tell Tracy and the rest of the family. I'm not sure how we're going to tell Mom and Dad. They know he doesn't feel well—back pain, shoulder pain. Somehow we have to take it from that to, "Oh yeah, all those tests Andy took, well, they came back, and he has about four to six months to live. Can you pass the potatoes, please?" My stomach is in knots, and I find it very hard to breathe. Every four or five breaths, I have to take a deep inhalation. I'm feeling light-headed and nauseous.

I start to make a mental list. I have to get all of Andy's medical records from Dr. Killjoy, and we have to find him the best doctors. I stop at the health food store, and Andy asks what we're doing there. "Look, Andy, you can kiss your old life good-bye. I wasn't kidding when I said we're cleaning up your diet. That starts now."

He pleads, "No, not now. I just want to go home."

I insist. "Andy, wait in the car. I'll be in and out."

He gives in. "Just hurry, please!"

Within minutes I walk out of the store with two green drinks, one for each of us, and a double shot of wheatgrass for Andy. I get in the car and hand him his drinks. He gives me a weird look and asks, "You expect me to drink this? And what's this in the tiny cup?"

I explain, "That's wheatgrass, loaded with nutrients and powerful antioxidants to boost your immune system." I sound like a frigging infomercial.

"Where's yours?" he asks.

I smile and say, "Oh, I can't drink that stuff. It has a strange effect on me. Leaves me feeling wired like I've drunk a whole pot of coffee." Actually, I hate it. It has this disgusting aftertaste that he'll be burping up for days. "Just drink it, Andy. All at once, like a shot of tequila."

"Don't I wish!" He laughs. Great to hear him laugh. He drinks it down. "Damn, Cass. That has got to be the worst thing I've ever tasted!" he exclaims. The grimace on his face is priceless. I'm grimacing right along with him.

"Sorry, Andy," I say understandingly. I've heard there are people who like this stuff. My opinion is it's impossible to like it; it smells like freshly mowed grass and manure. If people really liked it, they'd be serving it up in twelve- and sixteen-ounce servings, but instead they give you a choice of one or two ounces, with or without a barf bag.

We head back to Andy's house. I do ask myself why, but I don't ask myself why him because, really, why anyone? Cancer, stage IV. Not I, II, or III. IV, advanced, incurable…terminal. Andy doesn't even smoke. He's only forty-six. I'm having a hard time wrapping my mind around it. He and Tracy are planning on marrying next year. He has a whole life ahead of him…or had. I can't even imagine what life would be like without him. Our nightly talks while I make dinner, our runs on the trails, morning cups of coffee, and lunches at our favorite cafés. The laughter—no one makes me laugh like Andy, except maybe Mark and Joey. We get each other. I miss him already. I feel a huge lump in my throat, and for his sake I try to fight back the tears long enough to drop him off. But it's no use. The tears start streaming down my face.

I'm wearing my sunglasses and pray Andy doesn't notice. I don't want him to know just how terrified I am. He has to believe; he just has to believe.

Looking out the passenger-side window, he asks me if I watched Jon Stewart last night. I can't answer. "Cass?" he asks again. I still can't answer. "Hey, Cass, what's—" He looks over at me and notices that even my shirt is wet from my tears. He comfortingly rubs my shoulder and says, "Hey, remember what you said—we're going to find the best doctors. I'm going to clean up my diet and walk and do yoga with you. I'm even going to drink that green shit. Remember, Cass. Remember what you said? We're going to fight this."

Nodding my head, still crying, I manage to get out a few words. "Yeah, Andy, I remember, and we are. We are. I love you, Andy. I really, truly love you."

"I love you, Cass. Now knock this off, and let's talk about something else."

Trying to smile, I nod in agreement.

*

*A*ndy and I live minutes from each other, same community different neighborhoods. I drop him off. He and Tracy have been living together for about six months now, but she's not home. I tell him to call me if he wants us to tell her together. He says he will but thinks it will be all right. As I drive away, I feel like running as far away from this as possible. I want to drive away, far, far away. I have to pull over. I take my sunglasses off and start crying again, only this time with a primal sound I've never heard come out of me. My hands are on top of the steering wheel. I can't control the sound, the tears, the ache that's so deep inside me. I begin to slam my hands on the steering wheel, shouting, "Shit, shit, shit!" repeatedly. I finally manage to pull myself together long enough to drive home.

I pull up to our driveway, open the garage door, and see Steve's car. I'm so happy he's home. I pull into the garage, turn off the car, and just sit there paralyzed. I can't move. After a few minutes, Steve—he must've heard the garage door open—comes to see what's taking me so long. He sees me sitting there, head reclined on the headrest, staring off into space, no tears now. He immediately knows something's wrong.

He opens the car door, pulls me out, and softly says, "Come on, Cass." Then he just holds me as I start crying again. Joey and Lance come running to the garage. Steve puts his hand up and motions them away.

"Cancer, Steve. Cancer." I sob. He holds me tighter.

"Oh, Cass. I'm sorry, baby. I'm sorry."

I burst out, almost shouting, "Stage four lung cancer. Incurable, terminal."

"Oh God!" he says. I feel my knees almost buckle. "I got you, baby. I got you," he says lovingly.

We go inside, and my cell phone rings. It's Mark. I hand the phone to Steve. He answers, and I hear him telling Mark about Andy. He hangs up and tells me Mark's on his way over. I sit on the couch, and Steve comes and sits next to me, putting his arm around me as I curl my body into his, almost in the fetal position.

Mark's the only one who knows about the attraction I have toward Daniel. Andy, who I tell just about everything to, doesn't know. I know Andy would completely disapprove—and with good reason. Mark's one of the few people I've ever met who doesn't judge me. He guides, listens, and cares with an open heart. Even if I'm headed for disaster, he knows everyone's going to do what they want to do regardless of what anyone else says. He simply says, "Cass, if you fall, I'll be here, maybe not always to break the fall, but always to help you pick up the pieces." I'm the same way with him. That's why our relationship works so well. It's the closest to unconditional love I think I could have with another person who's not my child. Let's face it, regardless of what anyone says, most relationships are conditional and judgmental. When I hear some of my women friends gush and say, "Oh, my husband loves me unconditionally," I think, *Yeah, let's have him find you in bed with another man and see how fast his love becomes conditional!*

I also love how close Mark and Andy are. They hit it off right from the beginning. They used to golf together before all of this and go on runs. Andy knows how much Mark cares about me and my family, and he appreciates that. They make each other laugh and have inside jokes that I am not even privy to.

L ater Mark lets himself in and walks over to the couch where Steve and I are sitting. Steve instinctively gets up, and Mark takes his place, holding me tight. Steve tells me he's going upstairs to tell the kids. I nod my head.

For a long time, we don't say anything, and then Mark says, almost whispering, "Whatever happens, Cass, we got you. You understand? We got you. You, we, all of us will be OK, no matter what," he says again. "No matter what. You hear me?"

I nod my head and begin sobbing even more as I grab his shirt and bury my head into his chest. "I can't do this, Mark. I can't!"

Mark lifts my chin and says to me sternly, "You can, you will, and you already are." He gets up and pours us both some Scotch. I don't usually drink hard liquor, especially in the midafternoon, but Mark says it'll ease my nerves. I drink it down.

"Easy there, Cass," Mark says as he drinks his down as well and pours us some more.

"I shouldn't, Mark. I have to go to my parents' house later and tell them."

"All the more reason," he says, laughing a bit.

"Right," I say, smiling.

Steve comes down with the kids, both of them with eyes red from crying. I put my arms out, and each one takes an arm. I put my arms tight around them.

"Oh my God, Mom. What's happening? What's happening?" screams Joey.

"Life is happening, baby girl. Life," I say soothingly as I kiss her head. Lance is crying softly on my shoulder. "It's going to be OK, L. I promise you that. It will be OK."

Lance asks me, "Mom, are you going to lose your smile?"

I let out a little laugh and tell him, "Of course not, my angel. How can I ever lose my smile when I have you and Joey in my world?"

"Hey," I say to both of them, "look at me. No matter what happens to Uncle Andy, we're all going to be fine. Sometimes we'll cry, sometimes we'll be sad, but we'll also laugh, be happy, and yes, Lance, smile."

Joey asks, "Is he going to die, like soon, Mom? Be honest, Mom, please?" she pleads.

"Joey, your Uncle Andy's very sick, but he's tough and he's going to fight as hard as he can to beat this. None of us know when it's our time, but in the meantime we have to help him and each other get through this. If he or anyone else we love passes before us, we'll honor their memory by living our best lives always. Do you both understand what I'm saying to you?" They nod their heads. "Good," I say. "Now go pick up your rooms. Mark, if it's OK with him, is going to hang out with you guys while Daddy and I go to Grandma and Grandpa's and tell them what's going on." I look up at Mark to see if that's OK. He's standing and smiling, his arms folded across his chest, and nods his head in approval both of me and at staying.

Five

*A*ndy calls and tells me he doesn't want to be there when I tell Mom and Dad. I can't blame him. I don't want to be there either. "That's fine, Andy. I understand. I'll take care of it. Have you told Tracy yet?" I ask.

"I just told her. She's a mess," he says sadly.

"I'm sorry, Andy. Really sorry. Give her my love, and I'll call you after we leave Mom and Dad's."

"Hey, Cass, can you ask everyone not to call or come over tonight? Tracy and I just want to be alone and have a chance to take this all in."

"Of course, Andy. I'll make sure no one will bother you tonight, but I'm sure they're going to want to see you tomorrow," I respond.

"That's fine. Thanks, Cass."

"Love you, Andy. Talk to you soon."

"Love you, Cass."

*S*teve's already called William and Allison and asked them to meet us at my parents'. William just agreed, but of course

Allison had to ask a million questions. Steve doesn't have much patience for that kind of stuff and said to her, "Look, we're all meeting there at six-thirty. Either be there or not. I'm not discussing this over the phone."

We decide to call my parents a few minutes before we get there so they don't kill themselves with worry. They are not used to impromptu visits from us. "Hey, Mom. Me and Steve want to stop by for a little bit. Is that OK?"

She responds happily, "Yes, yes. Is everything OK? Did you eat? Do you want me to make you something? We have plenty left over from dinner."

I lie. "No, Mom. We already ate. We'll be there in a few minutes."

"OK. See you soon, dear." I should really tell her not to call me dear, but now isn't the time.

We get there a few minutes before six-thirty and wait in our car for William, Aamina, Allison, and Kyle. "Cass," Steve says rubbing my shoulder, "we are going to see this through. I am here with you every step of the way. Just tell me what you need. I want to say everything is OK, but things like this are never OK. But we will face it together, and we will get the kids through it together."

"I know, Steve. It's so much to take in; I can't even believe what's happening."

They all arrive right around the same time. William puts his arm around my shoulder as we walk up to the door and says, "What's up, Cassandra?"

I say, "Let's talk when we get inside. I only want to say this once."

I use my key to go in. My dad's in his usual black leather reclining chair, and my mom's standing next to it. When they see all of us, they know something's wrong, very, very wrong.

"What's going on?" my mom asks, almost in a panic.

Allison says sarcastically, "Well, at this point, only Steve and Cassandra know, so maybe they will enlighten us soon. The suspense is killing us. What, you two getting a divorce or some-thing? Do we really need a family meeting for that?"

My dad, not looking at Allison, says sternly, "Enough, Allison. Where's Andy?"

We all sit down. I begin. "Andy's at home, Dad. He's not doing real well—"

He interrupts with a look of concern on his face. "Is this about Andy, the tests he took?"

"Yeah, Dad. This is about Andy. His tests came back." I know better than to tiptoe around things with my father. "His tests came back," I say again. "All the pain he's been in, his back, his shoulder, the weight loss, well…that's because he has tumors in his back and shoulder, and they found a tumor in his lung as well." I look over at William. His face is white, just like Andy's was.

"Cancer?" William asks, shocked.

"Yes, lung cancer," I respond quietly.

My dad looks at me and says intuitively, "There's more, more you need to say, isn't there?" I can't even look at him anymore; the heartbreak on his face is killing me. "Cassandra?" he asks again firmly.

"Dad, the doctor said he may only have like four to six months, but there's no way he can know that. We're going to find a differ-ent doctor, better doctors. Andy's strong; he can beat this," I say desperately, trying to give him, everyone, hope. Then I hear this scream that scares the crap out of me. It's my mom. She's scream-ing at the top of her lungs and falls to the floor.

"No, no, not Andy, not Andy. Why is this happening to me? No, no, no! What did I do to deserve this?"

I think, a bit insensitively, *There she goes again, making it all about her.*

Allison and Kyle to the rescue—they fly into action, trying to pick her up off the floor. She resists, they insist, and she keeps resisting, banging her fists on the floor.

My dad finally says to her, "That's enough. Get up, and let's talk about this rationally."

William can't speak, but I see his face is now red and he's about to cry. Aamina is already there. I look away. I won't cry in front of them. I have to be strong.

Allison is frantic. "We have to go over there. We have to go to Andy's," she says.

I reply, "No, Allison, he doesn't want to talk or see anyone tonight. Leave it till tomorrow."

"What?" she shouts. "Are you kidding me? We need to be there for him right now!"

I patiently respond, "Yes, but this isn't about what we need. This is about what Andy needs, and right now he wants to be alone with Tracy." My mom is still hysterical in the background. "Look," I tell everyone, "we need to be there for Andy in any way he needs, not in the ways we think he may need. Monday morning I'm going to start looking for the best cancer medical team we can find, even if it's out of state, whatever it takes. We have to look beyond the statistics. Even if we look at the statistics, there are people on the other side of the poor prognosis who survive past the expected time. We have to hang onto that and believe that."

William's hands are on his face now, hiding that he's wiping tears away. I look away again. *Don't cry*, I keep telling myself.

Allison looks at me and with anger says, "Where do you live, Fantasyland? This is advanced lung cancer. It's in his bones. This isn't a splinter we're talking about."

Steve begins to say something in my defense, but my dad interrupts and says with anger, "Allison, sit down. I'm sure your sister understands the seriousness of the situation! Cass, do whatever you have to do. We're all here to support you and Andy. Money is no object. Let us know what we can do and how we can help."

I guess it's sort of implied that I'll be steering things, considering how close Andy and I are. My dad puts his head down and starts to cry. I can't see my dad cry. I go outside to his beautiful garden that he's so proud of and sit on a bench under the orange tree. I love the smell of orange blossoms; they bring me back to cherished childhood memories with Andy. I can't breathe again. I just can't breathe.

William comes out and sits next to me. "What the hell?" he finally says.

"I don't know, William. I don't know," I reply. We hold each other and cry.

⁓

The next couple of weeks are filled with gathering records, meeting with doctors, and trying to find the right fit for Andy. There's this one doctor at a cancer center that I have a really good feeling about, but it's hard to get in to see her. I talk to her appointment coordinator many, many times and do some serious schmoozing, and after several attempts she agrees to at least take Andy's records and present them to Dr. Babichev. "When can you get his records to me?" she asks.

"Now, now. I'll be right down," I say excitedly. "Please, my brother is in so much pain, and so far we haven't found a doctor we're comfortable with."

Reassuring me, she says, "Bring them down, and I'll see what I can do."

I reply, "Oh wow. Thank you, thank you!" doing the assumptive close I learned from Steve.

⁓

A few days later I receive a call from Dr. Babichev's office, and we get an appointment for the very next day. I call Andy, very excited, and tell him we'll be seeing her the next morning at seven-thirty. "You gotta get your butt up early, Andy. I'll be there at six-thirty. I have a good feeling about her, Andy. I really do."

He responds not very enthusiastically, "That's great, Cass, really great." I can tell he's still in so much pain. The pain pills take the edge off but really don't help that much.

We arrive at Dr. Babichev's office at around seven twenty, and surprisingly, we're called in almost on time at seven-thirtyfive. Andy's weighed in; he's five foot eleven and down to 142 pounds. The nurse takes all his vitals. All is good there. A few minutes later the doctor walks in. Her hair is light brown, very thick, and frames her face, heavy like the mane of a lion. *I could help her with that*, I think to myself. She walks over to Andy, puts one hand on his shoulder, and says with a Russian accent, "Hello, Andy. I'm Dr. Babichev."

Andy, looking up at her from the exam table, says, "Nice to meet you, and thank you for seeing me." He's always such a gentleman, and everyone who meets him gets his sincerity and sweetness on the spot.

She comes over to me and says, "You must be the sister, the very persistent sister."

"Yes," I reply, "that would be me, Cassandra. Nice to meet you, and thank you."

She begins, "I've looked over all your records, and yes, this is lung cancer that has spread to the bones in your pelvis and shoulder. I'm sure you've already been told that because it's spread beyond the original site it's considered advanced and therefore inoperable. I'd normally start chemotherapy right away, but in this case, with all the pain you're in, we have to address that first. I'd like for you, when we finish here, to walk over and meet with one of our radiation oncologists. We've already made that appointment for you. Radiation first to shrink the tumors that are causing you so much pain and discomfort, then we'll begin chemotherapy, aggressive chemotherapy. You'll go through six cycles, one every three weeks. It's a combination of three different types of chemo drugs to help shrink the tumor. After around the third cycle, we'll do another CAT scan and PET scan to see what kind of effect it's having on the tumor in your lung. After chemo I'd like to drain the fluid that's in the lining of your lung. I'd first like to see how much the chemo reduces it."

Wow, I think, *this person is prepared.* She's not fumbling through his records like she's seeing them for the first time. That's what most of the other doctors we met with did. She's keeping everything simple, and not once has she said "terminal" or "palliative."

Andy asks the same question he's asked every doctor we've met with. "How much time are we looking at?"

She responds, "If I could tell you that, I wouldn't be a lung cancer doctor—I'd be a famous and rich psychic. But seriously, I don't know, Andy. What you have going for you—and I know this might sound strange—is other than the cancer, you're in very good health. You don't come to the table with emphysema, high blood pressure, diabetes, or any other illness that could complicate things further. Also you're young and strong, so you should be able to tolerate chemo better than others facing this disease. I have a quite a few patients, and one in particular, who've lived way beyond anyone's expectations. One of my patients is going on his fifth year, despite a prognosis of only few months. Everyone is different. We just have to take a wait-and-see approach."

She walks over to him, puts her hand on his shoulder again, and says compassionately, "I have many drugs in my arsenal. If we see something isn't working, we try something else. Let's also start you on a stronger, more effective pain management program, at least until you're done with radiation. I'd like to order an MRI of the spine and brain just to make sure all is OK there."

Andy smiles, and for the very first time since he was diagnosed, I see hope in his eyes. Yes, hope!

We thank her and head over to radiology. The radiation oncologist, seeing how much pain Andy's in, schedules the appointment for two days out. We'll go every day for two weeks at six in the morning. I'm elated when we walk out of there. I can't wait to call my dad and tell him we have our doctor, our team of doctors, and there's hope. There really is hope.

Six

I haven't been to yoga in over two weeks. I am already tired from all the doctors, hospital visits, and constant phone calls from everyone asking about Andy. When I get home, I check my email and see an email from a woman I met in yoga, Angie. We've become friends to some degree and have had tea a couple of times together. She's very close to Daniel and Cheryl. I read Angie's email:

Hi, Cassandra. Haven't seen you in a while and was just a little worried. Is everything all right? We miss you!

In the six months I've been going there, I've met some really sweet people; we've become a little clique of sorts. I'm really touched by her email. I respond with this email:

Hi, Angie. Thanks so much for your email. I haven't been well. My brother has been diagnosed with advanced lung cancer. As you can imagine, I've been very preoccupied and busy with that. I hope to get back soon, if even for just a few days a week. Thanks again for thinking of me, and hopefully I'll see you soon. Please give everyone my best. Cassandra

Later that evening, I get a response from Angie, expressing how very sorry she is and asking me to let her know if there's anything she can ever do, from grocery shopping to helping with my kids. *How very thoughtful,* I think. I'm really touched by her email. I also notice an email from the studio. My heart flutters a bit. Could it be from Daniel? Well, whom else would it be from?

Dear Cassandra, I hope you don't mind that Angie told Daniel and me about your brother. I can't tell you how very sad we are to hear this. We're holding you and your family in our prayers. We've also put the monthly series of classes you purchased on hold for however long you need. We hope to see you soon. Until then, all of our best. Love and light, Cheryl and Daniel

I write back, thanking them so much for their thoughts and prayers and for extending my series. I can't help but be a little disappointed there wasn't an email from just Daniel. Out of sight, out of mind, I guess.

*start making dinner, feeling a renewed sense of hope. Maybe Andy can beat the odds and live much longer than expected. I have no illusions, but who knows? Every day they're finding out new things and coming out with different drugs. It also helps that Tracy's now cooking super healthy for Andy and making him juices every day. We can at least try to keep his immune system strong so he can better handle the side effects of chemo and all the other drugs he's taking and may have to take.

Steve has a meeting tonight so won't be home until late. It's just the kids and me. Lance comes running down to see when dinner will be ready. L doesn't walk into rooms; he runs, glides, floats, but never walks into a room. "Soon," I tell him. I love cooking. It's sort of a passion of mine. Dinnertime is my time. I put on some music, go out to my herb garden, pick whatever herbs I'm using for that evening's meal, pour myself a glass of red wine—blends are my favorite—and unwind. Cooking is like a moving meditation, just like yoga.

It's taken me several tries to grow my herb garden. For a long time, every time I tried, everything died. I could never figure out what I was doing wrong. My dad, who has this incredible green thumb, would try to talk me through it each time—he even set the whole thing up for me once—but it was no use. One time I called him and said, "So, Dad, I tried again with my herb garden. Almost everything died again, but you'll be proud to know my rosemary is thriving and doing so well!"

To which he replied, "Cass, rosemary can survive a nuclear holocaust."

"Really?" I said, surprised and disappointed. Many, many tries later, I finally got it.

My cell phone rings. I don't recognize the number. *Probably one of the parents from school,* I think. I answer, and the voice on the other end says, "Hello, Cassandra?"

"Yes," I reply, not sure who it is.

"It's Daniel." I'm speechless, and my heart begins to beat faster. "Cassandra?" he says.

"Yeah, yeah. Daniel, hi. I guess I just—well, wasn't—"

Thankfully he interrupts because I can't seem to get a coherent sentence out. "Is this an OK time?" he asks.

"Yes," I say. "Just making dinner." I take a big sip of wine.

"I know Cheryl sent you an email from us and I—we—me…I mean, I just want to tell you how sorry I am about your brother. I know from hearing you talk about him how much he means to you. I want you to know if you ever need anything, you can let us know."

Well, the "us" certainly took the wind right out of that sail, I think, smiling. "Thanks, Daniel, and thank you both for putting my series on hold. That was very kind," I say formally, especially after he used the *us* word. There's an awkward silence as I wait for him to reply.

"Cass?" Did he just call me Cass, and did my heart just skip a beat as he said it, and did I just not correct him? "If there's anything I can do"—he emphasizes the "I"—"you have my number now. Just call me. If you ever feel like talking, call anytime."

"Thanks, Dan." Yes, I said Dan. "That really means a lot to me, and I will."

"OK, Cass. Enjoy your dinner and have a good evening," he says sweetly. Then he adds, "Hopefully we'll talk again soon."

"You too, Dan. Thanks for calling." As I get off the phone, I'm feeling so happy. Happy he called, happy to hear his voice, and happy that, while I may be out of sight, I'm not out of his mind.

Seven

Andy just finished two weeks of radiation. The radiation oncologist says sometimes it takes some time afterward to really notice the results, but he's already in a lot less pain. He's eating better, walking better, and able to stand for much longer periods of time. We're all so excited about his progress. About a week after his last treatment, he says, "Hey, Cass. Let's go over to the lagoon and go for a walk."

"Really?" I ask him, excited and surprised.

"Yes, let's go!" he exclaims.

"Now that's what I'm talking about, Andy. Let's do this!"

I can't contain how proud I am of him. We walk, talk, and laugh, just like old times. He walks slowly, but he's walking. I ask if he wants to take a little break, but he insists he wants to keep going. I think about telling him about Daniel—I mean, it's innocent enough—but change my mind, worried he might judge me.

After our walk we go to our favorite restaurant and have lunch. I'm in heaven having this time with him again after what already feels like a lifetime of pain and frustration. The conversation is light and easy, just the way we like it. Andy's smiling and content, and that's all I need. He begins chemo next week, and if anything terrifies Andy more than cancer, it's being nauseous and throwing up. I keep telling him not to worry; they have drugs for that. The chemo he'll be receiving is strong, but Dr. B, as we affectionately call her now, says he won't have hair loss, so that's good. Before we knew that, he asked if I'd shave my head in solidarity with him like he hears some people do.

"Shave these signature locks? Hell no!" I responded.

He laughed and said, "I didn't think so."

⌒

*I*t's been over three weeks since Daniel's phone call, and there isn't a day that goes by that I don't think about calling him. I'm too afraid. I'm not sure how to begin a conversation like that. I think, *What if Cheryl is there? What if he was just saying that to be polite but really didn't intend or expect me to actually call?* I try to think of a good reason to call, but I don't have one. I keep hoping he'll call again, but I know the ball is in my court now. Or is it?

Again, he could've just been being nice and saying what everyone has been saying to me: "I'm here for you. Let me know if you need anything. I'm praying for you." And so on and so on. *Worst of all*, I think, *what if I call and he doesn't answer?* Then it's just out there, just hanging, and I'm powerless and vulnerable. I know I wouldn't leave a message, but he'd see the missed call from me. Ugh, that would be way too exposed for my comfort level!

Mark keeps saying, "Would you just call already? You're making me crazy. It's not like you're calling and saying, 'Hi, Daniel. Wanna get naked?' It's a phone call, for Christ's sake!"

Steve is working late again tonight, and both kids are at friends' houses. I'm pacing around my bedroom, anxious, trying to muster up the courage to call Daniel. I finally go to my contacts, where I've already added him, go to the Ds, and there it is. I click on his name, and it begins dialing him. I quickly press END. *Oh God*, I think, *that was close.*

"Stop, Cass. Get it out of your head," I say out loud. "Do not make the call. Don't do it!"

Most people think when you start speaking to yourself like this, you're trying to talk yourself out of something. The reality is you're doing the exact opposite. You're talking yourself into it but somehow trying to make yourself feel better so that once you have done whatever it is you shouldn't be doing, you can always tell yourself later you made every effort not to do it. It's just a game we play with ourselves—unsuccessfully, I might add, because in the end it's the same result, regardless of intention.

I do it. I make the call. Damn! It goes to voice mail. I don't leave a message. I knew I wouldn't, and I'm really hating myself for making the call. He must think I'm some psychotic stalker, calling and not leaving a message. Yuck! That's exactly how I didn't want to feel, vulnerable and exposed.

"Smooth move, Cass!" I say out loud. Now when I do go back to yoga, I'm going to have to find another studio. How can I possibly face him? I'm lying on my bed. "Stupid, stupid, stupid!" My yell is muffled by the pillow I have over my face. My phone rings. I jump up and look at it. It's Daniel! Do I answer? Should I let it go to voice mail? Maybe I don't have to change studios after all. I answer calmly, "Hello?"

"Cass?" Aww, there he goes again calling me Cass. I smile.

"Yeah, hi, Dan."

"Sorry I couldn't answer your call. Um, it was just that Che—" I can tell he's starting to say "Cheryl" when he stops himself. "It just wasn't the best time, but now is good. Can you talk?"

"Yes, it's fine for me now. I'm not really sure why I called. I guess I just wanted to talk to you." Oh great, now I'm sounding like a song lyric! I try to redeem myself. "I just wanted to see how you are." Not much of a save, but it's all I've got.

"I'm doing well. More importantly, how are you, and how is your brother?" he asks.

"He's doing so much better. The radiation therapy has really helped with the pain. We even went for a walk, a fairly long one." I can't contain my excitement. "He did so well, Dan, so well! Sorry, it's just so great to see him doing better."

"Wow, don't apologize. I'm so happy to hear that and to hear you sounding so well."

"There's still a long road ahead. He starts chemo next week, and I'm sure that's going to be really hard on him," I say, not wanting to be overly optimistic.

"Just take things one day at a time, Cass. Things will be all right," he replies thoughtfully.

"How are things at the studio?" I ask.

He hesitates and responds, "Not the same without you." I know what I want to say but don't think I should, so I say nothing. "Did that make you uncomfortable?" he asks me.

"No, it made me feel good," I respond, saying what I wanted to say a moment before. "Do you mean it?"

"Yes, Cass, I mean it. When I'm teaching I keep waiting for you to walk in, even starting classes a minute or two late hoping you'll make it. When I practice, I always hope the person putting a mat down beside me will be you."

I finally realize the feelings I've had for him are mutual. Mark's been telling me that all along, but I was never entirely sure. "That means a lot, Dan, really," I reply.

"When do you think you'll be back, Cass?"

"I'm not sure. My whole world seems to be revolving around my brother right now. I have to get him through chemo," I tell him.

"You also have to take care of yourself if you expect to take care of anyone else. Yoga will help."

I know he's right, but I don't know if I have the strength right now. "Yeah, maybe, Dan. Maybe one day soon I'll be back."

Then he asks tentatively, "Hey, Cass, don't take this the wrong way, but would you be open to maybe getting together for tea one day this week?"

I'm taken aback, not sure what to say. I want to say yes. That would be such a sweet distraction from all this heavy stuff I've been going through, but on the other hand, that's really tread-ing the line. I'm curious about what he means by "don't take this the wrong way," so I ask. It's obvious he isn't prepared to answer that. I guess it's rhetorical—what it really means is, "Take this exactly the wrong way because what I'm asking you is wrong." He's at least honest and says he's not sure what he meant, maybe that what he was asking was a little out of bounds.

I let him off the hook and say, "I think I'd like that."

He replies, surprised, "Really? How about Friday morning?"

"Friday works," I answer.

"Where would you like to meet, Cass?"

"We could meet at this café down the street from my house, then maybe we can hike one of the trails close by?" Not likely we'd run into anybody from yoga, and as far as any of my neigh-bors are concerned, Steve and I keep to ourselves. Even if we did run into someone, I'd just introduce him as a friend.

"Sounds great, Cass. Text me the address. How about nine o'clock?"

"Perfect," I respond.

⌒

The next day I call Mark and tell him I called Daniel. "What a relief!" he exclaims. "Now we can finally put that to rest. Cass, you were seriously driving me nuts with the should-I-shouldn't-I routine. So, what are you up to today?"

I ignore his question and say, "We're meeting Friday for tea at the café down the street." There's a long silence—a very long silence. "Mark, say something!" I implore.

"Cass, think about what you're doing. That kind of takes things out of the studio and to a different level. It's one thing to have an innocent flirtation or even talk on the phone occasion-ally. I mean it's exciting and could even spice things up between you and Steve, but meeting him? I don't know." Of course, he makes perfect sense.

"I know, Mark. Everything you're saying is true. I don't know why I feel so drawn to him. I get so excited when I see him or hear his voice. He intrigues me, and right now he's like this sweet distraction where I don't have to think about cancer, chemo, death, all of it," I say, pleading my case.

"Cass, you have to really think this through. If it was just getting together with someone from yoga, male or female, and nothing else, there isn't anything wrong with that, but you two, you guys feel something for each other. You're very physically attracted to each other. Just how far are you going to take this? First it's flirting a bit here and there, and then a phone call or two, and now tea. What next?"

"That's it, Mark. I wouldn't ever take it further than that. I guess I'm just curious more than anything, curious what he's like outside of the studio, curious if I'd still feel that desire and attraction toward him, even curious what he looks like in clothes."

Mark laughs at the last part. "Well, my sweet Cass, do what you need to do, and I'll be waiting with bated breath to hear every detail." He adds, "Be careful, Cass. I don't know this guy, and I hope he's not taking you for a ride."

I reply, "I will, Mark. Don't worry."

That Friday morning, I put on a pair of jeans and a T-shirt with trail shoes. I drop the kids off at school and make my way back to the café. When I get there, I start thinking more about what Mark said and start to second-guess myself. This shouldn't be happening; I know that. I turn off my car, take a deep breath, and walk into the café. To my surprise he's already there. He's also wearing jeans and a T-shirt, and his hair is down. I've never seen his hair down, and I like it. I like it a lot. *This certainly doesn't help things*, I think, smiling. He gets up, walks toward me, and gives me a long hug while quietly telling me again how sorry he is about Andy and everything I'm going through. I practically melt in his embrace. He smells wonderful—it's not cologne. If I had to describe it, it's sort of a fresh vanilla, sandalwood scent, nothing overpowering, subtle and delicious. This is the first time we've ever really touched except for the adjustments he gives me in class or the gentle brush or touch on the shoulder or arm.

"I've never seen you with your hair down before," I comment.

"No? So what do you think?" he asks, shaking it out a bit.

"I like it. I really like it," I reply with approval.

"What would you like to drink?" he asks.

"Jasmine green tea," I reply.

I reach for my wallet, and he says, "I think I can handle this one." I smile. He orders and comes back with two teas. "Thanks for meeting me, Cass."

"Thanks for asking."

Daniel says pensively, "Let's just get something out of the way."

No, no, I think, *let's not be getting things out of the way. Let's keep things in the way.* "What do you mean, Dan?" I ask, hoping this can stay light and not get too heavy.

"Um, nothing, forget it," he responds. Done, forgotten. Works for me. There's a lot to be said for forgotten moments in these sort of situations, not that I've been in many of them, and none since being with Steve. "I think about you a lot, Cass."

Hey, what happened to, "Um, nothing, forget it?" Can we get back there please? "You do?" I ask him. OK, that was a pitifully poor comeback. *You idiot, Cass, of course he does. Otherwise he wouldn't have said it.*

"Yeah, I do," he says.

I seriously can't think of anything to say, at least not out loud. I could say, "I think about you, too, like, all the time, even sometimes when I'm making love to my husband." But really, what purpose would that serve? I say the only safe thing I can think to say: "That's very sweet, Daniel." Ouch! We can take me out back and flog me later for that ego buster.

"'That's very sweet, Daniel'? Really, Cass?"

I love it; he's calling me out on that! Now that takes balls. Most guys would just take the perceived rejection and walk away with their tails between their legs. "Honestly, Dan, I'm not sure what to say. I mean, obviously I think about you too, otherwise I wouldn't have called and we wouldn't be sitting here. It's just hard to talk about or say out loud," I reply sincerely.

"Well, that's better," he answers. "Do you want to introduce me to some of your trails now?"

"Yeah, I do. There's this great hike not too far from here, but we have to drive. It's about four miles up the trail and back. Do you have time for that?" I ask him.

"I do," he replies. Turns out he loves hiking as much as I do.

He follows me in his car to the trailhead. We park, and I'm really happy to be out, away from hospitals, doctor appointments, and the phone calls from everyone every five minutes asking me how Andy is, even after they've just gotten off the phone with him. This is wonderful. I miss this.

We start heading up the trail; it's a challenging hike. The trail is rough and steep on the way up. We talk about the different hikes we've done. Turns out he's a serious hiker, not just day hikes but camping-out hikes, some for days. One of his favorites is White Oak Canyon in Virginia.

"Not the toughest but definitely one of the most beautiful," he says. "There are six waterfalls, wood bridges over pools of water—the scenery is just beautiful. And if you go in spring, it's loaded with all these incredible wildflowers," he says passionately.

He's also done many hikes in Yosemite, including Half Dome, as well as the Grand Canyon and Mount McKinley. Another one of his favorites is Superior Hiking Trail in Minnesota; it goes from Duluth, Minnesota, to the Canadian border.

"Cass, there are all these waterfalls and rivers that run through a forest of aspen, maple, balsam, birch, and some other trees—I can't remember all of them right now. Anyway, the beavers use them to build these massive dams. You'd have to see it to really get the enormity of it; it's unbelievable, just unbelievable." I'm smiling listening to him. His enthusiasm is so refreshing and making him more attractive by the minute. "How about you, Cass? You ever camped out?"

"No, just day hikes for me; I don't really care for camping," I reply.

"What's your favorite day hike?" he asks.

"I'd have to say anything in a rain forest. I've been to Costa Rica a couple of times and love the cloud forest hikes. The trees and ferns seem to rise up to infinity; there's every kind of orchid you can imagine, with waterfalls and glorious pools of water. Another favorite of mine is in East Maui, where the Seven Sacred Pools are. There are more than seven, of course; that's just what it's become known as. There are waterfalls that seem to appear and flow out of nowhere. You haven't lived until you've stood underneath one of those waterfalls after a long day of hiking." He's smiling staring at me. "What?" I ask.

"You," he answers.

"Me what?" I ask again.

"You everything. Your hair, your eyes, your smile, your yoga, your passion, your compassion, the way you tilt your head to the side when you say something or ask a question with that sweet grin. Yeah, you everything," he says again. I grin. "See, there it is, the slight tilt of the head and the grin that gets me every time," he says joyfully.

Time has flown by, and I can't even believe we're up and down the trail already. Dan walks me to my car. My heart's pounding as I wonder how our good-bye will be. We stop at my driver's side door. I get my keys out of my pocket, hoping for a quick and safe escape. He takes my hand. *Oh no, please, let's just say our good-byes already.* "I had the best time with you, Cass." I'm silent. "Please don't say, 'Oh that's so sweet, Daniel,'" he jokes.

I giggle and say, "I had the best time with you, Daniel. I really did."

He gives me a kiss on my cheek that lingers a bit and says, "Let's do this again sometime and talk soon. OK?"

"OK," I say.

"Maybe one day soon you'll surprise me and show up at yoga."

"Yeah, maybe," I respond.

With that I get in my car and drive away. I had the ringer on my cell phone off, not that I could get great reception out here anyway. I check my phone, and I have what seems like a hundred missed calls and texts. I pull over and start to go through them: Mom, Dad, Mark several times, Steve a couple of times, Tracy three times, and a text from Tracy that says, "Call right away please." I panic and call her.

"Tracy, what's up? Everything OK with Andy?"

"I'm not sure, Cassandra. He says his calf hurts quite a bit, especially when he gets up to walk. I wanted to call the oncologist, but Andy keeps saying no, let's just wait and see if it gets better. It's not getting better." She sounds really worried.

"OK, I'm only about fifteen minutes away. I'm going to phone the oncologist on call at the hospital and see you in a bit."

I call and speak with a receptionist, who takes my number and says someone will get back to me shortly. I get a call back right away. I explain the pain Andy's having, and they tell me to head straight to the ER. It could be a blood clot. Oh shit! I'm feeling guilty I wasn't there earlier to take Tracy's call. I telephone Tracy back and tell her we have to go to the ER right away, to make sure they're ready when I get there. Tracy's personality tends to be a bit passive, which worries me when it comes to Andy and his health.

I get to Andy's, and they're waiting outside, Andy sitting on a patio chair. Tracy helps him up. He's walking on the ball of his right foot. I jump out of the car and open the passenger door to help him in. Tracy gets in the back. I barely say hello to either of them and start speeding down the road, wanting to get to the hospital quickly.

"Ah, Cass?" Andy says. "You mind slowing down? If the cancer or blood clot don't kill me, your driving will."

I begin to apologize. "I'm so sorry I missed your calls. I was out hiking, and the reception is really bad out there." Sort of true, right?

"Cassandra," Tracy says, "you don't have to apologize. We only started calling you about forty-five minutes before you called. I just panicked and kept calling. I should be sorry for scaring you."

We get to the hospital in record time. I pull to the front of the ER and drop them off. "You guys go and get checked in. I'll park and be right there."

I finally find a place to park and run to the ER. Tracy says they're checked in and are just waiting now to be called. I crouch down and place my hands on Andy's knees. "You OK, Andy?" I ask him, concerned.

"Yeah, Cass, just a little pain in my calf. Compared to the pain I had in my back and shoulder, this is nothing."

They call Andy's name. *Man, that's fast*, I think. The triage nurse takes his vitals and asks about all the drugs he's on. Andy keeps looking at me. I have them memorized down to the milligram. Then an administrative person comes in and asks if we have a medical directive. A medical directive—what's that? Andy shrugs his shoulders. I ask her what that is.

She says gently, "That's in case Andy can't make medical decisions for himself; he appoints someone to speak for him, to carry out his wishes." She hands Andy a folder, and he hands it to me. "Look that over, and if you have any questions, feel free to ask me," she says and walks away.

I start reading it. It's about what kinds of treatments you want and don't want at the end of life, how far to take diagnostic testing, whether you want resuscitation when the prognosis is very poor, and whether you're willing to be an organ donor. My eyes get blurry with tears. This kind of knocks it all home. This is important; everyone should have a medical directive whether or not cancer or any other life-threatening illness is involved, but just knowing Andy does makes it all too real.

I explain to Andy what it is, and he says, "Will you be my medical director, Cass?"

I laugh at his choice of words with a few tears dropping from my eyes and say, "Of course I will." I look around wondering where Tracy is; she's off in a corner crying. I walk over to her, give her a hug, and tell her it will be OK.

They take Andy back to an examining room and give him a gown to get into. I wait outside while Tracy helps him. She pulls the curtain back open, and I walk in. I hate the smell of hospitals; it's like bleach, linens, antiseptic, blood, and vomit all rolled up into one. It's also below zero in the room; I'm freezing. The cold temperature is supposed to ward off germs. I get it; if I was a germ, I wouldn't want to be hanging out in the Antarctic either. I sanitize my hands like every five minutes on those things they have hanging from the walls. I text Steve and explain to him what's happening with Andy and that he'll have to pick up the kids from school. He agrees and asks me to keep him updated. I decide to wait to call the family. No use worrying everyone until we know what's going on.

They take Andy back in a wheelchair to have an ultrasound on his calf and a chest CAT scan. Tracy and I wait in the examining room. Tracy says very seriously, "Cassandra, I want to marry Andy now. I don't want to wait."

Trying to lighten things up, I reply, "Well you might want to wait till he gets back from taking all those tests." She starts laughing and then laughing so hard she starts crying. I go to her side and hold her again. "Hey, Tracy, I think that's really cool. I think it's amazing; we can plan it together if you want. OK?" She can't respond, just nods her head yes.

They roll Andy back about forty-five minutes later. He looks exhausted. I know all this is taking a toll on him, but we still have a long road ahead of us. Chemo starts Monday, and that's going to have its own set of side effects. Word to the wise: never read the pamphlets they give you regarding the drugs and their side effects. I was up late one night reading about the cocktail they're going to be giving him; let's just say it's not pretty. You'd think with all these brilliant minds out there they could come up with something that isn't like Hiroshima and Nagasaki, destroying everything in its path. I'm hoping that the healthier way he's eating and juicing will help with the side effects and keep him strong.

The doctor comes in and says it's a blood clot, just like they suspected, and it's good we came in when we did. A blood clot can kill a person if not caught early enough. Let's go ahead and add that to the top of my already full guilt plate. As if climbing mountains with someone I've no business being with in the first place isn't enough, I almost killed my brother as well. Thanks, Doc, for that bit of trivia. I take a deep breath and feel very thankful that all is OK. Andy will have to start taking self-administered shots twice a day, once in the morning and once in the evening. I call William and explain the day's events—well, part of them anyway—and ask him if he could call everyone and let them know. I'm exhausted and don't feel much like explaining and reexplaining. He says yes and asks to talk to Andy. I hand Andy the phone.

~

After dropping off Andy and Tracy, I decide to go to the café by my house for a tea and relax for a while before going home. I get a call from Allison, and I answer it. She doesn't even say hello, just starts yelling. "Cassandra, don't you think when things happen like this we deserve to be kept in the loop? Next time anything happens, you need to call us all right away. What gives you the right to withhold information from us? I didn't even know Andy was starting chemo on Monday. I knew it was next week sometime, but not Monday, and I don't even know what time. What's that about, Cassandra?"

I calmly respond. "Look, Allison, you want to be kept in the loop, then loop yourself in. I can't take care of everything I have to take care of plus Andy and babysit your needs at the same time. If you want to know what's going on, pick up the phone and ask. It's a very effective form of communication. Been around for years. Try it sometime." I don't wait for a response and hang up. This is the last thing I need after hours in an emergency room. She calls back, and I let it go to voice mail.

⁓

The next morning I call to check on Andy. Tracy answers and says he's sleeping and doing fine. He still has pain in his calf, but the doctor told us that it will take a couple of days to correct itself. I tell her I'm going to yoga but will have my phone on vibrate and will check it every so often, to please call if they need me.

"Cassandra, everything is fine. I'm so happy you're going to yoga today. Have a great class, and don't worry," she says warmly.

"Thanks, Tracy. I'll call again after class." I really like Tracy, and I'm so happy Andy has her back in his life, especially now.

⁓

I'm so excited to go to class. I've missed the heat, the yoga, and the way I feel after class. I'm also excited to see Daniel. I walk in, knowing he's teaching this class, and like our first meeting, his back is to me. I sign in and say, "Hi, Daniel."

He turns around with a surprised look on his face. He just stares at me for a few moments. Suddenly the surprise turns into a big smile. "Cass, you made it!" he says happily but quietly.

"I did, and that looks like pleasure to see me," I say, smiling back at him.

"You have no idea," he responds.

"Yeah, I think I do." I grin coyly and walk into the yoga room. I receive a beautiful reception, even from people I don't know very well. All the attention makes me uncomfortable. I'm so touched by everyone's kindness and well wishes. I place my mat down and can't wait for class to start. Daniel turns on the lights, and everyone stands. He walks straight toward me and says, "So nice to have you back with us, Cassandra," so people within earshot can hear him. It only sounds like a yoga teacher welcoming back his student.

"Thanks," I reply. "Good to be back."

He begins class, and inside I'm smiling. I love his classes and keep thinking about us, our hike, and the sweet things he said to me. The guilt has dissipated about Andy and missing Tracy's call. Everything worked out OK. I begin to build up a good sweat, and I start getting into the zone. I push myself and know I'll be sore tomorrow, but I'm here now, and who knows how often I'll be able to come once Andy starts chemo?

We're in Separate Leg Forward Bend when Daniel comes over and gives me an adjustment. "Shift your weight more forward," he says, gently placing his hands on my hips and pulling them toward him. "Now pull even harder on your heels and lengthen your spine." He glides his palm down the length of my back. "There it is. You got it. Nice. Feel the difference?" he asks soothingly. *Yes, Dan, I feel the difference.*

He says something interesting to the class. "Desire causes suffering. Wanting something you can have or something you can't have causes suffering, so the goal is to become desireless."

I get it. That's Buddhism 101. What I don't get is why he says it now considering it contradicts our mountaintop experience. We both want something we can't have, and here we are, both knowing better, reaching for it. This interaction between Daniel and me, if we allow it to escalate, will cause suffering. There shouldn't be any more meetings outside of the studio. This has to be stopped before it gets out of hand.

We move on to Camel Pose, a very powerful back-bending pose that can stir up many emotions and discomfort. Backbends tend to do that, while forward bends are more comforting and soothing. When we come out of the posture, Daniel says, "If you're feeling emotionally overwhelmed, with either joy or sadness, love or fear, tell 'em what it means, everyone."

Most of the class responds loudly and in unison: "Accept and transcend!"

Daniel replies, "That's right, accept and transcend."

Eight

Andy's completed three cycles of chemo, and he has one every three weeks. He's very, very tired and takes a lot of antinausea medication. It breaks my heart to see him this way. The weight he'd put on he's lost again and then some. His face is ashen and gaunt. How is he going to handle another three months of this? Tracy's been amazing. I'm really not sure what he'd do without her. She's only working part time now. I'm there when she works; we don't like Andy being alone during this time. When she comes home, I pick up my kids and take a break.

I've been able to make it to yoga about two to three times a week. It gives me such relief from all the worry and fatigue I feel. Daniel and I talk on the phone about two or three times a week and text almost every day. I tell myself every time is the last time, but it never is.

Steve seems to be working more than usual; he comes home late most nights. I warm his dinner, and he goes right up to his office and works some more. Maybe Daniel's my escape and work is his. When I try to bring it up, he gives me the standard, "I'm doing the best I can, Cass. I'm only one person," and so on. I miss Steve, and we seem to be growing apart. The tension is sometimes really thick, but we just ignore it and move on about our lives. We don't even have sex as much as we used to. In all fairness, there's so much going on, and he's taken on a much bigger role with the kids since I'm not always around like I used to be.

This is our new normal. Hospitals, doctor visits, sometimes spending more time at Andy's than at our own home. It's not just going in for chemo; he also has several appointments in any given month. He has to have regular blood tests, a standing monthly appointment for another infusion of medication to keep his bones strong, B_{12} injections, bimonthly meetings with his oncologist, trips to the pharmacy. Since he's completed his third cycle, we're waiting for the results from the latest CAT scan and PET scan. The wait is excruciating.

*D*aniel and I decide to meet at the café again—so much for becoming desireless and stopping things before they get out of hand. On my way there, after dropping the kids at school, I get a call from Dr. B's nurse case manager. (Andy and I agreed that all calls go through me. I'm his patient representative. All we want him to concentrate on is getting better and keeping his strength up.) My heart is practically pounding out of my chest; I'm so nervous.

"Cassandra, hi. It's Elaine." No other introduction is necessary. I've talked to them so much I feel like I know them all personally.

"Hi, Elaine," I reply, barely breathing.

"Cassandra, the results from the CAT scan and PET scan are in. Dr. Babichev asked me to call you with the results." That's a good sign. If it was really bad news, wouldn't the doctor have called herself?

"Yes?" is all I can say.

"The tumor in his lung has shrunk by thirty percent. The fluid in the lining of his lung has reduced as well. The PET scan is clear; the tumors in his pelvis and shoulder did not indicate anything active, and no new areas lit up."

"That's good, right, Elaine? I mean really good?" I exclaim.

"Yes, Cassandra, that's very good. It means he's responding well to the chemo."

"Oh my God, Elaine. That's amazing. Thank you."

I can't get off the phone fast enough to call Andy. I tell him the good news, and he doesn't say a word. Nothing. Tracy takes the phone and says, "Cassandra, I'll have him call you back. He's kind of emotional right now. The results weren't so good, huh?"

"No, no. They were great, Tracy. Great! The tumor's shrunk by thirty percent, fluid is down, and the PET scan came back clean!"

"Oh my God, Cassandra!" she screams. "Thank God!"

"Tracy, I have to call my family and tell them. I'll call you guys later!" I call William and get the same reaction as with Andy: silence. It's all very emotional for everyone. I ask him to call Allison and my parents; he's become my conduit to them. My dad ends up calling me anyway, and I have to repeat everything again.

"Dad," I always ask, "didn't William just talk to you?"

"Yes," he says, "but I want to hear it from you." I think he thinks nothing is real until I say it. Who knows? I call Steve, but he's in a meeting with some new investors.

I get to the café, and for some reason I have a hard time finding parking. Something must be going on at the school across the street. I finally find a spot and start walking toward the café. I see Daniel down the street; he must've had a hard time finding parking as well. He sees me and smiles. I start walking fast at first, then running toward him, happy and obviously excited. I race into his arms and hug him. He twirls me around.

"Is this pleasure to see me?" he asks, laughing.

"No—well yes, but no—I mean, Andy's results came back, and everything is good, really, really good, better than expected," I say to him, my hands on his shoulders and his hands on my hips.

"Wow, Cass, that's incredible, just incredible!" he says, sharing my excitement. We just look at each other, my heart so full of joy for Andy. I'm practically in Daniel's arms, and I feel like I want to kiss him. I break away thinking, *That's too close. Be careful, Cass. Remember what Mark said. First an innocent flirtation, then talking on the phone, then some stolen moments outside of the studio. What next? Nothing*, I say to myself, *nothing. Just this. And just this is perfect; just this is enough.*

The café is packed. Daniel says, "Cass, let's forget about tea, head east, and drive toward the mountains."

"That sounds great. Let's do it," I respond enthusiastically. We take his car. The drive is so beautiful; the road is lined with pine, cedar, and fir trees. I open my window and put my head out. The feel of the wind on my face, my hair blowing, and the smell of fresh, clean air is magnificent! Like Daniel always says in class, "Feels good to feel good!" I have a huge smile on my face.

Daniel pulls into a picnic area and parks the car. We get out and start walking. "You look beautiful, Cass!" he says exuberantly.

"*You* look beautiful, Dan!" I respond playfully. We walk over toward a creek. There are tadpoles swimming everywhere. I tell him how when Andy and I were little—he was probably around nine, and I was five—we'd go to this pond by our house and catch tadpoles and put them in plastic bags. We'd bring them home and put them in this fountain we had in our backyard that was filled with water. Andy said if we watched them long enough we'd see them turn into frogs. One night we stayed out for hours. Andy had a flashlight, and we just kept staring at them, waiting for them to become frogs. We never did see it happen.

One evening Andy woke me up and said, "Cass, get up. Get up." I got up, and he whispered, "Do you hear that?"

"Hear what?" I said, groggy.

"Quiet, listen. Don't you hear the croaking? That's some of our tadpoles. I just know it!"

"Really?" I asked him, wide-eyed.

"Yeah, Cass, some of them are frogs now. Isn't that cool?"

"Wow, really cool, Andy!"

Daniel says, "Cass, you still have this innocence about you, even though lately you've been through so much. You aren't letting it make you bitter or jaded."

"I don't know if I'm *not letting* it make me bitter or jaded—that sounds like a conscious effort—I just don't look at it or feel about it that way," I reply.

"That's the innocence I'm talking about." He grins.

His hair is down, and as I'm looking at him, I want to feel it, touch it, run my hands through it. I want to touch him, feel him, smell him, experience him. I know it's impossible, but the desire is there anyway. Where did this come from? Where did *he* come from? *Why* did he come? He takes me by the hand, and we start to walk toward a nearby trail.

I pull my hand out of his and say, "That's probably not a good idea."

"What, not in the mood for a little trail hike?" he replies.

I give him a look and say, "You know that's not what I mean."

"I know, Cass. Of course I know," he says, amused. We start walking again. "I don't just want to hold your hand, you know?" He smiles again, looking over at me. He continues, "Do you ever wonder—I mean, think about me in that way?"

Must we go there? I think. Instead I say, "Please, Dan, don't ask me questions like that."

"I guess you do then." He looks at me flirtatiously. I turn away, shaking my head. "You know you do, Cass. You can admit it. No one out here but us and the trees, and they're not talking," he says, looking up at the sky and trees with his arms outstretched to his sides, palms facing up.

"Come on, Dan. Stop," I respond, pretending to be irritated.

He changes the subject. "What are your kids like, Cass?"

"Oh no. Don't get me started on my kids. I'll never stop," I reply.

"Really, get started. I'd like to know."

"Well, Lance—we call him L—is truly an old soul. He's only twelve, but he has things figured out better than most adults I know. He's just so easy to be with; anyone who meets him falls in love with him. His teachers all adore him. He loves music from old rock to new rock but nothing mainstream. He can draw and read for hours. He practices kung fu and is so beautiful to watch; he has excellent form and is so graceful. One of his favorite books is *Lord of the Rings.* He also loves Woody Allen movies.

"Joey is fourteen and is a ball of fire. She has so much passion and zest for life. Any adventure you throw her way she's up for. Very independent and secure with who she is. She's extremely protective of her brother, more than I am even. When we're out at a store or mall I don't worry, because I know she's got it. I have to rein her in a bit, though, because I want Lance to be independent and not fear the world.

"Both kids are musically talented, Lance on the guitar and drums, Joey the piano. Our house is always alive with music; we rarely watch TV—" I stop and shake my head. "See, I told you. Don't get me started on my children.

"No, no," he says reassuringly. "I love anything that gives me more insight into you."

I show him pictures of them on my phone. "Beautiful kids, Cass. Joey is gorgeous, and Lance looks exactly like you, same dark curly hair, same eyes, everything!"

"Thanks, Dan. How about you? What are your kids like?"

"Well, when I met Cheryl she had two kids from a previous relationship. They were really young, and their father was out of the picture. I raised them, and they're a hundred percent mine as far as I'm concerned. My son, Brandon, even looks like me. He's twenty-one and a musician—plays guitar, keyboard, and saxophone. He lives and breathes music. He's struggling but following his passion; I admire that about him.

"My daughter, Leah, is nineteen and in her second year of college at the University of Michigan. She's very intelligent, reserved, and extremely determined. When she sets her mind to something, she follows through. She wants to be a doctor someday, either pediatrics or obstetrics." He shows me pictures of his kids.

"Wow!" I exclaim. "You sure your son isn't biologically yours? He does look just like you, even wears his hair like you."

He smiles proudly. "You should see his yoga practice, puts his old man to shame."

I smile and say, "Yeah, I seriously doubt that! Your daughter looks like Cheryl," I continue. "Very pretty and with such a sweet smile." It feels very strange mentioning Cheryl's name. I immediately regret it.

"They're good kids—can't complain," he adds.

"Speaking of kids, we need to head back. I have to pick mine up soon," I say.

⌒

The drive back to town is quiet but not uncomfortable. We talk a little, but we don't feel like we have to talk, which is nice. He pulls in next to my car. Whatever was going on by the café earlier is over; hardly anyone is around. I'm not really concerned about our good-bye this time. I'm certain Daniel understands this is as far as I'm willing to take things.

"Thanks, Dan, for a really great day!"

I start to get out when he gently grabs my arm and pulls me toward him. "Come here, Cass."

"Dan," I protest, pulling away slightly.

"Cass, come here. Don't worry." He pulls me closer, puts his hand on one cheek, and kisses me on the other. He lingers longer than last time and says softly, "You always smell so good, Cass."

"Lavender," I whisper, our cheeks still touching. I want so much to kiss him. "I have to go," I say, pulling away. As I start to open the car door, I hesitate, turn, and face him. I stare into his eyes that I love so much, lean in, and give him a kiss on the cheek. He smiles sweetly and brushes his hand along my face. With that, I leave.

Nine

$\mathcal{A}$ndy finished his last three cycles of chemo four months ago. It kicked his ass, but he's doing so much better. The scans showed even more improvement and that all is stable. The fluid in the lining of his lung will still have to be removed, mostly because when he moves in certain ways it bothers him. He's on maintenance chemotherapy that doesn't have nearly the side effects that the cocktail of three had. The last eleven months or so since he was diagnosed feels like a lifetime.

As the weeks go by, I can see Andy getting stronger. He has color back in his face, and he's putting on weight. He's not nearly as tired as he was, and we walk and jog almost every day. His goal is to run a 5K. He's very passionate about running and golf. We signed up for a race with William for three months out. Andy says he'll finish it even if he has to crawl across the finish line. We consider ourselves in training. I do yoga with him at his house, especially poses to strengthen his spine. We also do breathing exercises to help his lungs and his mind. He looks forward to our sessions.

I call him, as I do every night, to see how he's doing. He says, "Guess what."

"What?" I ask.

"I ran two and a half miles today without stopping."

"Are you kidding me? That's fantastic! Why didn't you call me to go with you?"

"I don't know," he says. "I guess I just kinda wanted to see if I could do it alone."

"That's great, Andy. Next time, you and me, though, OK?"

"You got it, Cass!"

～

*M*y yoga practice is consistent, four to five times a week. Daniel and I still call or text one another almost every day and see each other outside of the studio now and again. Despite the obvious sexual attraction, I've managed to keep things relatively platonic. I know Daniel wants to take things to the next level, but I am not willing to go there. I guess I am satisfied with the attention and companionship our relationship gives me. Also, if this ever came out, it would be easier to say nothing physical ever happened. He's talking about possibly opening a second studio.

Steve and I are basically occupying the same space. It's almost like we are living separate lives; when we talk it's mostly about the kids, work, mundane stuff. We don't talk about the obvious distance that's growing between us. We also have a lot less patience with each other; we bicker and are defensive over the littlest things. I guess that's better than the apathy I feel creeping up sometimes. Apathy is very dangerous in any relationship; it usually signals you better do something quick or kiss the relationship good-bye. Mark has suggested we try counseling, but with everything I have going on, I don't have the inclination or energy for that. I've never been one to talk about relationships; I just prefer having them. This past year has been physically and mentally exhausting for both of us. Maybe now, with Andy doing better, things will improve.

I hear the garage door open while making dinner and feel myself tensing up. I used to be excited when Steve came home;

now it's a mixture of dread and anxiety. It's not even that we fight—at least that would indicate passion. It's just sort of this passive-aggressive thing we both do. The bickering is tedious and, quite honestly, boring. He walks in, gives me a kiss on the cheek, and asks me how my day was and where the kids are.

"Fine, upstairs," I tell him, barely looking up.

"Cass, I'll be in my office. I've—"

I interrupt him; I can't hold it in any longer. "Wait, wait don't tell me. A couple of deals to put together, a couple of calls to make, and you're really buried this week. Did I cover it all, or am I missing something? Oh yeah, I'll call you when dinner is ready. There, I think that about covers it, unless you'd like to add something new and exciting to this old, tired, worn-out routine we go through most nights of the week."

He starts to say something, and again I interrupt him. "Don't say anything, Steve. Let me help you out: you're doing the best you can, do I know what our nut is, the kids' school alone is over fifty thousand a year, and you're only one person. See how convenient this is? You don't even have to be here for this conversation, not that you're here anyway, even when you *are* here!" I say, throwing the knife on the cutting board as I walk over to mix the stir-fry on the stove.

"Dammit! Who do you think I do all this for?" he responds, livid, slamming his briefcase down on the kitchen counter. "I do it for you and the kids. I'm trying to take care of my family, and all you can do is stand there and be snide and sarcastic. You know, Cassandra, sometimes you can be a real nightmare. I've tried really hard to be there for you this past year since Andy's been sick. I picked up the kids whenever you asked me to, helped out around the house, and did whatever I could to help. You have been so distant and angry with me lately, I don't know what to do."

"First," I say sharply, slamming a drawer shut, "stop hiding behind the, 'Who do you think I do this for?' crap. I used to buy into that. Not anymore. You do it for you. You get off on it.

It's what makes you feel good. It's your ego boost. That's fine. I could deal with that *if* when we're all together you could at least pretend you're listening to us and fake being interested in our lives. Do you know how many times at dinner Lance or Joey will ask a question before you come back from whatever deal it is you're working on in your head and realize they're asking you something? How do you think that makes them feel?

"Forget me—hell, I'm used to it. I can handle it. I know when you're tuning me out even before you do. Joey will mention one of her best friends' name, and you always act like it's the first time you're hearing it. Lance will tell you about a project he's working on at school, one he's been talking about for weeks, and again you act like it's news to you. These are your kids, Steve, and you only get one shot with them; that's it. There are no do-overs. As for helping out during this last year, well excuse the hell out of me that my brother got cancer and life has somehow managed to inconvenience you."

Joey and Lance come downstairs. "Mom, is everything all right?" Joey asks timidly. We've always made it a policy not to argue when the kids are around, so this is clearly scaring them, especially Lance.

"Take your brother and go upstairs, Joey," I say firmly. Joey takes L outside instead, where they can't hear what's going on.

They've felt the buildup of tension at the dinner table. Kids aren't stupid; they're very perceptive and intuitive to the world around them. This blowup between Steve and me has been a work in progress, and I can feel it's going to get worse. I go on, now angrier than ever. "I hear you on the phone with your employees, clients, and investors, and you hang on every word they say."

He interrupts, "That's business, Cass, business."

"What are we, Steve? Just your goddamned family, that's all! How about hanging on every word *we* say? How about discovering who and what we are and what we're becoming? Hey, you know what? It's your loss, because you're missing out on some really incredible moments."

He's seething at this point. He makes a fist and looks around like he wants to punch the wall or something. "You act like I'm some kind of monster. I'm doing the best I can. What the hell do you want from me?"

"Everything, Steve! I want everything, not the material stuff you give us to ease your guilty conscience. I want your heart, your soul, and I want some depth."

"Depth?" he asks. "What's that supposed to mean?"

"Exactly!" I shout.

His phone rings, and to my astonishment, he answers it. "Hey, Jennifer," he says, moving into the other room. I hear him laugh and then say something like, "Yeah, I didn't see that coming either."

Jennifer is his office assistant. She's calling after hours on a Friday? What the hell? Has he completely lost it? And this familiarity he has with her, when did this begin? I hear him laugh again and feel like I'm going to throw up. I'm furious. How dare he take her call in the middle of what I think is an important and pivotal conversation in our relationship?

I turn the stove off, toss the salad, and grab my purse and keys. I walk over to Steve, take the phone out of his hand, and press END. I tell him dinner is ready and for him to feed the kids.

"Where are you going, Cass?"

"As far away from you as possible," I yell.

"Is this your idea of working things out?" he shouts.

"No, actually, that thought hasn't even crossed my mind!" I toss him his phone and add, "Here you go. Wouldn't want you to keep Jennifer waiting!"

I get in my car and start to leave. The kids are sitting on the curb. I roll down the window and tell them, "You guys go inside now. Dinner is ready, and Daddy is waiting."

"Where you going, Mom?" Lance asks with a little fear in his voice.

"I'm just going out for a bit. I won't be long. Go on, you two, do as I say." I watch them go in before driving away. I want to call Daniel but decide not to. In the state I'm in, heaven knows what I'd let happen. I call Mark instead.

"Hi, Mark. Is this an OK time to drop by?"

"Hey, I was just getting ready to call you and see if I could stop by your place, so yeah, come over. Are we having wine?"

"No," I reply, "get out the Scotch."

"Uh-oh. OK, I'll have it ready. Hey, drive carefully. See you soon!"

⌒

I get to Mark's, and he has the Scotch ready to go. "Look, Cass," he says, "if you're going to be drinking Scotch, I'm not letting you drive home tonight." He knows I'm a lightweight when it comes to hard liquor.

"OK, I'll text Steve and let him know I'm staying over. I need a break anyway," I say. He also has appetizers ready, fruit, bread, crackers, vegan cheese for me, and a few other things, always the perfect host. I grab a piece of bruschetta and explain everything to him.

"Jennifer? Really?" he says. "She's nothing on you, Cass. Maybe you're taking it wrong. I mean, you couldn't hear the other end of the conversation."

"Mark," I say, frustrated, "I didn't have to hear the other end of the conversation. Now in retrospect, I'm realizing her calls are very frequent and at strange hours. It was his demeanor with her. And the fact that in the middle of our argument he takes her call like I'm not even there. I've been so distracted with Andy and taking care of him, I guess I kind of just brushed it aside."

Mark says as gently as he can, "Cass, sweetie, let's just keep things real. You've been distracted in another direction as well; let's just call him Daniel for argument's sake. Maybe that's also why you didn't see what—if anything—is happening with Steve and Jennifer."

I hate even the sound of that: "Steve and Jennifer"! "I know, Mark. I know." The Scotch is hitting me now. "OK, let's change the subject. What about you? What've you been up to?"

"Oh, you know, the usual, working, paying the bills, yoga... and I slept with Greg last night."

"What did you say?"

"You heard me. I slept with Greg last night."

"Mark, are you kidding me? You're supposed to be getting over him!"

"Baby steps, Cass, baby steps," he says reassuringly.

"Baby steps, are you serious? It's been a year and a half, Mark. Don't you think, instead of these baby steps, it's time to take one giant leap for humankind and end this thing once and for all? He uses you. You know that. He comes around and toys with your emotions, then you don't hear from him for a month or two, and it's the same thing all over again. It's like the movie *Groundhog Day*, only in months or something like that—you know what I mean."

Mark laughs and pours us more Scotch. I'm munching on some crackers. "It's the last time, I swear, the very last time. I told him that. You should've heard me Cass; he knows I mean it this time. I could see it in his eyes. I swear I even saw a tear just dying to come out."

I burst out laughing. "Really?" I ask. "A tear, a single tear, just stuck there, suspended in time? I can just see you sitting there rooting for him. 'Come on, Greg. You can do it. I believe in you, man. Let it roll. Let it roll!'"

Mark's laughing hard now. "I'm so weak, Cass. It's pathetic."

Mark and Greg were together for over five years and were even planning on marrying, and then Mark found out Greg was living this double, even triple life. He lied and cheated on Mark so much, a few of them Mark's friends. We can laugh about it now, but Mark was devastated at the time, just devastated. There's no love lost between Greg and me. When I run into him, it's hard for me to hide my contempt.

I look over at Mark as I lie back comfortably on his couch, a nice Scotch buzz going now, and say, "Hell, who am I to judge either one of you, Steve included? Look at me. What makes me any different from Greg? And if you're weak and pathetic then I'm even worse. I'm married, and every time I'm with Daniel I say it's going to be the last time, and it never is."

Mark says, "First, you're nothing like Greg. He gets off on hurting people. What he did to me was premeditated and happened with many people and all the time. And you're weak, maybe. Pathetic, no. It's just like this sweet distraction you were talking about. Doesn't make it right, but it's nothing like what Greg did, not even in the same universe. Damn, Cass, you haven't even kissed Daniel." Mark, always defending me, no matter what. I must've done something very right in my life to have a friend like him.

Mark and I are both feeling no pain at this point from the Scotch. I smile and say to him, "Haven't kissed him *yet*."

He looks at me, surprised. "Yet?" he asks.

"Yeah, yet. Man, I want to, Mark, maybe just to get it out of my system. I'm dying to know what it would be like."

"From what you've been telling me, it would be great—really great—but wouldn't it just suck if after you have all this sexual tension—loving his touch, his smell, his sweetness, and his tenderness—he turns out to be one of those kissers who leaves you feeling like the Hoover Dam just exploded all over your face?"

With that I completely lose it and can't stop laughing. Neither can Mark. This is exactly the distraction I needed.

⌒

*L*ate the next morning, nursing a hangover, I head home. It's Saturday, so Steve and the kids will be home. I don't want to see Steve, but what choice do I have?

I walk in and there he is, sitting on the couch, still in the same shirt and slacks from the day before, looking like he hasn't slept much. "Cass, we have to talk," he says.

"I have nothing to say to you," I respond. I can't even look at him.

"Nothing to say?" he repeats impatiently. "That's a bit juvenile, don't you think?"

"Juvenile?" I ask indifferently. "Yeah, if you say so."

I can tell Steve is trying to be patient but starting to get frustrated. "Cass, you can't just shut down every time we have a problem. All this sarcasm and hostility isn't getting us anywhere."

"Can't shut down? Watch me! What was that yesterday, Steve? What? We're in the middle of a conversation—argument—whatever you want to call it, and when Jennifer calls, you not only take her call, you start talking like Casanova. Your tone and demeanor completely changed, so sweet, laughing and carrying on. Really, how am I supposed to be feeling? Like I want to open up so you can twist the knife in even deeper? Not your finest moment, Steve! While we're on the subject, what is it between you two? Why this shift? And when did this happen? Please don't try to deny it. You know exactly what I'm talking about. Pretending otherwise makes you look like the fool, not me!"

He begins, trying to explain, "Jennifer and I've become friends, nothing else."

I look at him, completely baffled. "Friends? Really? Well, that kind of goes against your whole men-and-women-can't-be-just-friends theory, or do your theories change to suit your needs? And since when do you have friendships with your employees?"

"Cass, try to understand. These last few years—"

"Oh please," I interrupt. "Do not reduce our sixteen years of marriage and two kids down to the last few years. And with your assistant, no less? How cliché, Steve. How very, very cliché! Go ahead; have your little friendship. I hope it serves you well. Now I'm done talking." I go upstairs to take a shower, leaving Steve sitting there.

Ten

With less than two weeks until our 5K race, Andy's in great shape. He was always the athlete of the family, a natural if ever there was one. He ran cross-country in high school and was always the one to beat. We've been running regularly. He really hurts after our runs but says it's worth it to be out there again on the trails. William runs with us whenever he can and has been spending a lot more time with Andy.

The three of us go out together to run one of Andy's favorite trails. We call it the snake trail because once Andy and I saw a rattlesnake right there in the middle of the trail. We were running right toward it when Andy put his hand out in front of me and quietly said, "Stop, Cass. That's a snake up there."

Silly me, I told him, "No, Andy, that's a tree branch. Look, it's not even moving."

"No, Cass, it's a snake. And by the colors and the rattle, I think it's a rattlesnake."

Rattlesnakes are very common in our area. "Oh no, Andy. Let's go back," I said, frightened. He picked up a rock, threw it in the direction of the "tree branch," and sure enough, it slithered away, off the trail. But I was still scared. "I want to go back, Andy.

What if it's really pissed off now and is just waiting for us to pass by so it can spew its venom?"

Andy gave me a look like I was out of my mind. "Cass, I don't think snakes lie in wait or even think. My guess, it's all reactive and instinctual with them."

I was hesitant but agreed to move on, hanging onto Andy's arm as we walked slowly past the place where the snake had slithered into the woods. Once we passed it, I took off running, Andy right behind me. I think about what an interesting metaphor this is. I am helping Andy face his snake, the cancer, and he gave me the courage to move forward and face my fear of snakes. I guess we all have our snakes in one form or another. Do we become reactive and run away from them or intelligently move forward with courage and strength? That's up to us.

The three of us set out for our run on the infamous snake trail. William is in excellent running shape. William, Andy, and I are really getting into a groove now. We're running together, William hanging back with us. I can't believe how strong Andy is and how well he's doing. At around mile two, we're entering "the zone." All we can hear is the sound of our breath and our feet hitting the trail beneath us. There's this gentle warm breeze and it feels like the world's standing still, giving us a standing ovation while we run by.

Toward the end of the trail, Andy starts to kick it into high gear and runs faster and faster. William and I look at each other, shrug our shoulders, and start running after him. When we finish, we high-five each other, and I realize this is a run we'll never forget.

"I think I'm ready," Andy says, breathing heavily.

"You think?" William and I say almost at the same time.

William adds, "You're there, Andy. You're there!"

When I get home from our run, I'm so proud of Andy, not just for the run but for his strength and courage fighting this horrible disease. I decide to put it down in writing and send him an email. Late that night, I get a response from him:

Cass,

As far as I'm concerned, you're the kind of person I can say I envy and wish I were half the person of. Compared to you and the life you've led, I qualify as a lifelong member of the Couch Potato Society. Are you kidding me? Don't you remember when we talked about people that have such a passion for life, a love for life, and how it far supersedes anything else? Man, no matter what anybody said, you were doing it the way you felt was right and at any cost. It all paid off, Cass. We walk into the health food store, and people's faces light up with a smile as they greet you. Your husband is one of the best human beings I've ever met, and I don't say that lightly about anyone. Your kids are amazing. And you think that comes out of thin air? I think not.

I've written an email to the family that will go out to express my feelings toward all of them. This is just for you, however: I mean it when I say that without your help, I wouldn't be on the road to recovery right now. I'm truly overwhelmed at the sacrifice you've made to accommodate my situation. It's a *huge* sacrifice you're making, Cass, and I can't see anyone else making that kind of a sacrifice on another's behalf, so I want to thank you from the bottom of my heart. As things go along and I can handle more on my own, I hope to ease your burden and be more help. For now just know I love you and always have in a way you may not know or understand. Take care, Cass. See you tomorrow.

Andy

I respond with this:

Wow, Andy, I'll try to respond through a flood of tears and emotions. First of all, as far as I'm concerned, this is no burden and no sacrifice. I've received more than I've given in the past year and a half. I've felt more, loved more, cried more, and appreciated more than I have in my entire life. I have, for the first time, completely understood what unconditional love means and felt what true vulnerability feels like. I thought I understood what hope, strength, and courage were. I realize now that I had no clue. Every day I learn more about who I am, who you are, and how someday this will make us all better people. Believe me again when I say I've received more than I've given. Like that song says, "He ain't heavy. He's my brother." Well, you ain't heavy. You're my brother…and so much more.

I'd be lying if I said I haven't thought of running and hiding as far away from this as possible. The intensity of the emotions is overwhelming at times, but it's then that I realize those thoughts come from a place of fear. Things like this, especially this, need to be faced head on and with no shortcuts. All I ask is that you never give up and never give in. Nothing is insurmountable. I love you Andy and there isn't anything I wouldn't do for you. I want you to know that I have your back in this life and beyond, and I know you have mine. Much love to you always, Cass

On the morning of the 5K, I'm so excited to run. Steve takes the kids in his car and I pick up Andy and Tracy in mine. We meet William and the rest of the family at the race. It's overcast and cool, perfect running weather. This day reminds me of the day William and I ran a marathon together. He's run several marathons and even qualified for the Boston Marathon. I didn't actually run it with him. I was in the same race as him and about sixteen thousand other people.

Many of the people running in the marathon were in a group, all wearing blue, running to raise money for cancer research, some of them with their faces painted, wearing funny hats, Mardi Gras necklaces, and whistles. At the beginning of the race I found their enthusiasm entertaining; they were hooting and howling, blowing their whistles, trying to get the crowd excited. But by mile twenty I was ready to strangle this woman behind me with her necklaces and make her eat her whistle. *Nobody has the right to be this happy at mile twenty,* I remember thinking. *At least have some respect for the rest of us who are seriously thinking this is the closest we're going to be to death without actually dying. That is, assuming we don't die.* At around mile twenty-three, I saw what looked like a dead raccoon on the side of the road and thought, *That's going to be me, roadkill. They'll be scraping me up off the street soon.*

When you see marathon runners crossing the finish line with so much elation and jubilation, it's not just because it's over—although that's certainly part of it. It's because we're happy we're still alive! The first thirteen miles aren't so bad; anything beyond that is just masochistic and cruel. I couldn't walk for two weeks. I had to walk down the stairs backward because going down forward hurt too much. Cross that off the bucket list; I never want to do that again! Looking back I really appreciate, now more then ever, all those people with their whistles and horns running their hearts out for cancer.

William, Andy, and I are close to the starting line, warming up and stretching. I already feel myself getting emotional. I can tell Andy's nervous. He doesn't only want to finish—he wants to finish strong. But just Andy's making it to the starting line is a success in my book. I'm truly humbled by how much courage and tenacity it took for him to get here.

They call all runners to the starting line. Andy says to William and me, "Don't worry about me, guys. Just run your race."

William says back to him, "I have a feeling we'll be eating your dust."

The gun goes off, and we take off, nice and easy to begin with. We're all together. We can almost feel the weight of what we're experiencing with every step we take. This isn't any ordinary 5K, not for the three of us anyway. This is an entire year and half of ups and downs, fear, trust, sadness, joy, anger, hope, frustration, and delight. At around the one-and-a-half-mile mark, Andy picks up the pace. William and I stay with him at first, but then he starts picking it up even more. William is still with him, but I start to fall behind. I'm smiling and filled with a happiness like I've never felt before. Andy, stage IV lung cancer, is going to kick my butt! *You go, Andy. Have the run of your life,* I say joyfully to myself.

We come around a turn, and the finish line is in sight, about three-quarters of a mile down the road, people along the way cheering the runners coming in. I start to pick up my pace and try to catch up to William and Andy. I want to finish with them. They start to pick up their pace too. I'm close but not close enough. They cross together, and I'm about one minute behind, giving it all I've got. I see them at the finish line and hear them yelling, "Come on, Cassandra. Kick it in! Kick it in!" I do. I throw my hands up in the air, look up toward the sky, and cross the finish line. I run to William and Andy, and we all embrace, laughing and crying at the same time.

"You killed it, Andy. You killed it," I yell.

"Yeah, I did, didn't I?" Andy says proudly.

William joins in, patting him on the back. "Hell yes, you did!"

We walk over and grab bananas and waters at the refreshment stand. The rest of the family and Tracy run to Andy, hugging and congratulating him. There are moments in families when all is forgotten, all is forgiven, and there's this unity of love, this common denominator that prevails. Those moments are precious and few, but no matter. It's here now, and Andy's our shining star, our common denominator.

Eleven

A couple of weeks after the 5K, I get a call from Tracy. "Cassandra, there's something wrong with Andy's eye," she says, worried.

"What do you mean, something wrong? Is it his vision? Is it hurting him? What?" I ask.

"It's red and looks big," she says. "He says it hurts behind the eye."

I respond, "Look, Tracy, you guys get ready. I'm not going to waste time calling the doctor; let's head straight to the ER. That's probably what they're going to tell us to do anyway."

She agrees, and I head down to their house. I call Tracy as I come through the gate to their house so they can meet me outside. I pull up to the driveway, and Andy gets in the front with me. I can immediately see something is definitely wrong with his left eye.

"Hey, Andy, your left eye is looking really pissed off," I say, trying to be lighthearted.

"Yeah," he replies, "it feels really pissed off too."

We head toward the ER, and I ask him when this started. "The pain started a few days ago," he tells me, "but I didn't think too much about it because it wasn't bothering me that much.

Then last night and this morning it started to get more red and bigger, and the pain behind my eye is very intense."

As he's talking, I'm thinking, *Wow, can't this poor guy get a break? Seems like it's always something. He just ran the race of his life and still on a high from that...and now this.* My hope is that it's nothing serious and not related to the cancer. "Listen, Andy, before I get my ass chewed out, primarily by Allison, do you want me to call the family to let them know we're on our way to the hospital, or do you want to wait until we know what's going on?" I know what he wants before he answers but don't want Allison's wrath like last time.

"Let's just wait," he answers. "I don't want everyone coming down and making a big scene when it could be nothing."

We get to the ER and check Andy in. Now I can see more plainly just how irritated and awful Andy's eye looks. It's literally bulging and it's really red, almost purple on the eyelid. They call Andy back and take his vitals. He's running a slight fever. They take us to the exam room where Andy says to Tracy and me, "This isn't going to be good, guys. I can just feel it."

"Let's just wait and see what the doctor says. It could just be infected or something."

The doctor comes in, asks Andy a few questions, and looks at his eye with a little flashlight. He says he'll need to run some blood work and order an MRI of the sinuses and orbit.

Orbit, I think, sounds like something related to astronomy. "What's the orbit?" I curiously ask.

"It's the area around the eye," the doctor explains. OK. That makes sense since that's where the problem seems to be.

Two hours after Andy's MRI, we're still in the ER. Tracy and I are passing the time talking about their upcoming wedding. Andy had promised her they'd get married after the 5K, and now this happens. She's so excited talking about her vision of how it will be. It's bittersweet.

The doctor finally comes and in sits down, which, by the way, is never a good sign. He begins to explain the results. "Andy, somehow you've contracted retro-orbital cellulitis."

Why can't these guys ever speak in layperson terms? That would be like me talking to someone who's never done a yoga pose before and suddenly breaking out in Sanskrit. Andy logically asks, because it sounds like something out of a science fiction movie, "What's that?"

"It refers to the spread of an infection either from the sinuses or through the blood. We can't know for sure where it originated."

So, I'm thinking, *No big deal. Write him a prescription for antibiotics and we can be on our way.* If only things were ever that simple.

The doctor goes on. "This is a very serious infection that can be life threatening, and in your condition, we need to be even more aggressive. We're working on getting a room ready for you, and since you also have cancer, we'd like you to stay in the cancer ward. We have to keep a close eye on your blood counts and will have to monitor you regularly to see if the antibiotics are taking effect. We might have to experiment with a series of different antibiotics, but we can cross that bridge if it becomes necessary. You'll probably be here for a minimum of five days. It could be longer depending on how you respond to treatment."

The look on Andy's face breaks my heart. He can't believe what he's hearing any more than I can. My mind begins to drift as I think back to the day Andy was first diagnosed with cancer. It was about as unbearable as anything any of us could've ever imagined, but we didn't have time for *Why him? Why us?* because, again, why anyone? While this road we've been on has been filled with our share of rough patches, it's also been filled with so much love, joy, laughter, hope, and gratitude. I hope we can all learn to love deeply, laugh freely, forgive more, and get angry less. Right now we're all in survival mode and getting used to this life as our new normal. I personally have little time or energy for philosophical evaluations or digging beneath the surface to see how and if this is going to make me a better person.

I believe things in life happen to show us more of who we are. As far as Andy's concerned, watching him come so far and already beat the odds they put in front of him is remarkable. He chose to battle this on every front available to him. He immediately changed his diet and started juicing, practicing yoga, and taking daily jogs and walks. He completely and wholeheartedly committed to doing whatever he had to do to increase his odds of survival. For that, I'll always admire and respect him, more than I ever thought I could. That's not an easy undertaking for anyone, much less someone battling an advanced stage of cancer.

I hear Tracy saying, "Cass, Cass…" I look over at her, and she says, "Where did you drift off to? I've been calling your name. Andy's room is ready. They're coming to take him up."

"Sorry. OK. That's good."

On Andy's third day in the hospital, I stop by to drop off food for them and visit for a bit. Tracy meets me in the hallway and tells me she feels like she's getting sick, so I tell her to go home and I will stay with Andy. She doesn't want to leave and says she will just keep her distance. I try to convince her we can't risk Andy catching anything else.

"We are all here, Tracy, Mom, Dad, William, and Allison. Go home and get better so you can take care of him when he comes home. We will all take turns taking care of Andy and his food."

We are making all his meals because, well, simply put, hospital food sucks. I can't believe the crap they feed the people they're trying to heal. Hippocrates said, "Let thy food be thy medicine." Hospitals never got that memo.

Tracy's hesitant to leave. Poor Andy's getting increasingly despondent with each passing moment. One of my fears has been that one day his physical illness will become a mental one, and he'll stop fighting. For the past three days, he's barely eaten and has refused to get out of bed to walk around the ward. He's just lying there, hardly talking, staring at the ceiling, telling us how terrible he feels.

Tracy finally agrees to go home until she feels better, and I walk into Andy's room, hopeful he's feeling a bit better than yesterday. It's the same scene, only a different day. He hasn't shaved, looks awful, and is more depressed than I've ever seen him. I give him his oats in a thermos and tell him to please eat. He says he will later. "Andy, you've *got* to eat!" I implore.

"I'm not hungry, Cass. Get off my back."

"Fine, then let's take a walk around the ward, just a few laps," I plead with him.

"No, I'm too tired. I can't," he replies.

"Tired from what? Not from all the activity you've been doing, that's for sure!" I say, frustrated.

"Yeah, well, I'm just a lazy bastard," he answers defiantly. I back off, sit down, and read a book I brought with me. Andy watches TV or just stares at it—I can't be sure.

Around lunchtime, I take out the sandwiches and soup I made for us. He immediately says, "Don't bother with me—I'm not hungry—but you go ahead and eat."

That's it. I've had enough! I walk over and close his room door. I take his food and put it on the tray next to him. I go to the bathroom, get his toiletry bag, and hold it up. I say very loudly, "You want to die in this hospital bed, go ahead and die. Here is your lunch. In this bag you'll find some objects that have become quite foreign to you, so let me help you identify them. This is a toothbrush." I hold up each object as I name it. "This here, this is toothpaste. This stuff with string is dental floss, but you don't have to worry about that since it's typically used to get the food— that you aren't eating—out from between the teeth. Wow, look what else I found, a razor and shaving cream! Oh and look here. What's this?" I hold two objects up, one in each hand. "Don't be shy, Andy. Go ahead, just shout out the first thing that comes to your mind." Andy's glaring at me. "No, nothing comes to mind? That's OK. Let me help you out. This square thing is soap, and this in the plastic bottle is called shampoo. Imagine that! These are normally used to clean oneself. You look and smell horrible, and I'm not going to waste one more minute here watching you drown yourself in this ocean of self-pity.

"Look, Andy, if anything happens to you, there are going to be a hell of a lot of pieces to pick up, and who do you think is going to have to clean up that mess? Not you, because you'll be dead. This is a hurdle, Andy, one you can overcome. We must fight battles like this with courage and strength, not the way you're doing it, like a coward, with anger and fear. You know, you may not win this fight with cancer, but how do you want to be remembered—like you went down fighting or that you were brought to your knees by some frigging eye infection and decided to check out 'cause you were tired? I'm leaving now. I refuse to be a party to this!"

Andy just lies there shell-shocked for a minute or two. I'm gathering my things when I see him moving his legs like he's getting out of bed. "You know, Cass. You can be such a bitch when you want to be, sarcastic as all hell! I don't know how Steve puts up with you when you get like this!" he says angrily as he struggles to get out of bed. He grabs his IV stand and starts walking toward the door. He looks over toward me and says, "Well, you coming or not?"

"Yeah, I'm coming," I reply quietly.

"A real bitch!" he says again, now with a little smile.

We walk around the ward. We don't do a couple of laps; we do twenty. He has a few more choice words for me along the way, but I don't mind.

⟜⟶

*A*ndy's released from the hospital four days later and stays on oral antibiotics for three weeks, but he makes a full recovery. I think back still to our walk around the ward. He walked those twenty laps for every one of us who cares about him, loves him, and needs him in this world, a world that, for me, makes no sense without him in it.

Twelve

Six weeks after Andy is released from the hospital, he is happy and ready to marry Tracy, and we're all planning a small wedding ceremony and reception. It's a very exciting time. Tracy's father died about twelve years ago, she never had kids, and her mother, Elizabeth, and sister, Christy, have very mixed emotions about the wedding. On the one hand they're excited and happy for her, but on the other, they worry this will be too much for her if something happens to Andy. The way I see it, pain is pain. Married or not, she'll hurt and grieve the same.

William and Aamina have two beautiful acres in a more rural part of town, and they offer to host the ceremony and reception. It'll be a small, intimate affair, about seventy-five people total.

I meet Tracy, her mother, and her sister at a bridal boutique to look at dresses. She wants something simple, just like the ceremony. She begins to try on dresses, and she's glowing from the inside out. Tracy has that girl-next-door look. Her hair is sandy blond; she has blue eyes and is very fit. She goes to the gym regularly. I persuaded her to try hot yoga with me once, but she never went back. She said the next time she wants to experience something like that, she'll just douse herself with gasoline, light herself on fire, and do the elliptical—faster, easier, and less painful than the ninety minutes of torture I put her through. Clearly, it's not for everyone.

She tries on her sixth dress and it's obvious right away this is the one. She walks out in this very simple yet elegant dress that elongates and complements her petite figure. It's a strapless, long silk dress that kind of cinches high on her waist and then flows down to her feet. It accentuates her shoulders and arms that are so toned, who wouldn't want to show them off? She's just stunning, and her mom and sister tear up.

"Cassandra, do you think Andy will like this one?" she asks me.

"No, Tracy," I answer. "He'll love it!"

She starts crying from what I assume is a mixture of happiness and sadness. "It will be two years soon, Cassandra. Two years. And they told him four to six months, twelve at the most. Thank you," she says sincerely.

"Wow, don't thank me. He's doing it. You both are. No one is in the thick of it like you two are."

She smiles at me and says again, "Thank you, Cassandra."

"Cass," I correct her and walk over and hug her.

That evening, we're at home. Steve's upstairs, playing chess with Lance. He really has been making more of an effort with the kids and even me since our big fight. Every time he tries to explain this thing with him and Jennifer, I shut him down and tell him to leave it alone. I believe, in some ways, one of the reasons I don't want to hear it is because it gives my relationship with Daniel some justification. There's a part of me that thinks they crossed some lines they shouldn't have because Steve doesn't believe heterosexual men and women can be just friends. That's something we've talked about a lot. Those late nights at the office and the comfort and sympathy she offered him could've been taken further. Maybe someday I'll be open to hearing about it but not now. He can brain dunk this thing somewhere else. He can ease his guilty conscience to someone else, not me. We're still not communicating well, but things have gone from hostile to civil. The kids need us to be that way, and we need us to be that way. Sex is more frequent, but I think that's more the need to have sex for the physical release. We're both holding back emotionally.

I get a call from Daniel. I'm always happy to hear from him. "Hey, Cass. Can you talk?" That's the way our conversations usually begin.

"Yeah, but not for long," I respond.

"I was wondering if you want to take a drive up to the mountains tomorrow."

"Yes, Dan, I'd like that."

"Great, let's meet at the café around nine," he says happily. It's been quite a while since we've been alone.

"See you then. Good night, Dan."

"Good night, Cass."

I turn around and see Steve standing there. My heart starts beating fast. How much and what did he hear? Dan and I didn't say much. I start going over the conversation in my head, my side of it anyway. Nothing too incriminating, I don't think, but I did say "Dan" a couple of times.

"Who was that?" Steve asks.

Think fast, Cass, and don't fumble your words! I tell myself. "Zach's father wants to know about taking the boys paintballing this weekend." This is one of the few times I'm relieved that though Steve should know Zach and Zach's father—whose name is Allen, by the way—he's totally disconnected from that aspect of our kids' lives.

Considering all that's going on, he pretends to know exactly who and what I'm talking about. "That sounds like fun," he says.

"Yup, we'll see. I was kinda wanting to have this weekend with just us and the kids for a change," I say, exhaling the breath I've been practically holding for the past few minutes.

"Whatever you think," Steve replies.

That was close, and fortunately Zach *did* ask Lance to go paintballing this weekend, in case Steve brings it up to him. I really hate that I just lied to Steve. Up to this point, it's been only lies by omission. Even though it's pretty much the same thing, this feels different. I have a pit in my stomach and think about texting Daniel to cancel. I decide to sleep on it and make up my mind in the morning.

⟜⟶

The next morning after sleeping fitfully all night, I make up my mind I want to go. I rationalize to myself that if Steve can get up almost every morning, go to the office, and see his "friend" Jennifer, I can go see my friend, whom I do see regularly but only occasionally alone. I'm looking forward to seeing Dan. I sometimes think we really are just friends. It's been two and half years, and despite the flirtation and sexual innuendos, we've only kissed on the cheek. There is, however, this tremendous attraction and sexual desire that takes it right out of the friend zone. We also talk more intimately than friends talk, and we both know if things were different, we'd have been past the kiss-on-the-cheek stage eons ago. Our circumstances are what they are, and that's a simple fact of life. This—the way things are now—my conscience can live with. I don't know why; it just can. Anything more, and I don't think it could.

It's a chilly morning, and I wear a jacket. We get to the café almost at the same time and grab our teas and some snacks to go. We take Dan's car, and the drive up is anything but silent. We're talking like a couple of friends who haven't seen each other in years and are playing catch up. Even though we see each other quite a bit at yoga, we rarely get to talk, especially so freely.

I bring up this woman in his Saturday class who has these huge implants that are so big on her frame it's cartoonish looking. I remember thinking—when I was pregnant and nursing the kids and had my 38DDs—*Why would anyone pay for these?* It was so uncomfortable, my back hurt, running with them was a joke, and I had to forget about sleeping on my stomach. To each her own, I guess. Besides the implants, she's had so much work on her face it doesn't move, and her lips are unnaturally huge. She's a woman in her forties trying to look like a woman in her twenties or thirties.

"So, Dan, that woman in Saturday class—you know the one— she's usually in the back behind me, close to the window. The one with the ungodly sized breasts and lips, blond hair, bleached of course?" I ask him.

He tries to look confused, but the grin on his face gives him away. "I have no idea who you're talking about." He grins some more.

"Really, Dan, you know exactly the one. The one that between every set of postures moans and groans so loud it sounds like she's having an orgasm? Then she crumbles to her mat, moaning all the way down like a damsel in distress, while you run to her rescue and say, 'Are you OK? Would you like me to crack the window a bit?' To which she breathes very heavily and says, 'Yes, please.' That one, Dan."

"Oh, that one. You didn't mention the moans and groans earlier, so I wasn't sure," he says, teasing me.

"Well, in classes with other teachers I've taken with her, she's not nearly as vocal and only sounds like she's doing some heavy petting, not having a full-on orgasm like in your class. I thought you might find that interesting," I explain.

"Why, Cass, do I sense a bit of jealousy on your part? That's new, not something I've seen from you before!"

"Oh please, jealous? You've got to be kidding. Just making conversation!" I say defensively.

"Oh come on, Cass. I know jealousy when I hear it, and you're definitely jealous." He laughs. "What about that guy who puts his mat down so close to yours even when there's plenty of room? That blond guy. He always looks over at you and smiles."

I defend the blond guy. "Come on, he doesn't put it that close."

Dan gives me a glare me and says, "Hell, Cass, if he put it down any closer, you two would be practicing on the same mat!"

I laugh at that comment. "Who's jealous now?" I ask.

"Me," he says, agreeing. "At least I can admit it. I don't like it when guys in class are like that with you. I'm a guy. I know what it means," he replies protectively.

"I never knew that—I mean that it bothered you," I say, surprised.

"Well, now you do," he answers honestly. I'm actually flattered.

We get to the picnic grounds, and I'm really sleepy. I not only didn't sleep well the night before, but I haven't slept well in two years. Daniel parks, and I ask if we could just get in the backseat of his car and talk; at least we wouldn't have the console between us.

He asks, concerned, "You OK, Cass?"

"Yeah, I'm just really tired. I didn't sleep well last night. And I don't feel like going out where it's cold." We get into the back and share one of the energy bars we got from the café and finish what's left of our tea.

"Come here," he says sweetly, putting his arm around me and pulling me close to him. I rest my head on his shoulder. He brushes my hair with his fingers, and the next thing I know, I hear him whispering, "Cass, Cass, get up. Get up. It's getting late. You have to get your kids." I sit up, and for a moment I'm not sure where I am or what happened. "You fell asleep, and then I fell asleep," he says. "It's OK. Don't worry. There's time." I take a deep breath. I can't remember ever crashing like that. "Hey," he says, "we finally did it."

"Did what? I ask.

"Slept together," he says, kissing me tenderly on the forehead.

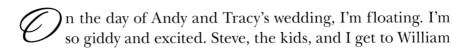

On the day of Andy and Tracy's wedding, I'm floating. I'm so giddy and excited. Steve, the kids, and I get to William and Aamina's early to help set up. Their kids are all home from work and college, and Allison and Kyle's kids will be there as well. It's one of the few times—except for some Christmases and Thanksgivings—our whole family will be together. William has an interior designer friend who helped decorate the yard. All the flowers are white, from calla lilies to peonies to white tulips. The white wood seats are set to circle the trellis in the center, the way an orchestra would be set up, only in a full circle. The trellis is draped in tulle and organza fabric. It's placed loosely, with some flowers scattered along it. The whole scene is out of a fairy tale.

Mark arrives, and I run and give him a hug and kiss. He's in charge of drinks, and I'm in charge of the food. We are having an open bar, and the catering company is considered to be one of the finest in the county. I am also in charge of Andy since I am his best man, and Christy, Tracy's sister, is the maid of honor. This is going to be a great day!

It's spring, Andy's favorite time of year. It's early, so it's a bit chilly, but there isn't a cloud in the sky, and the day should warm up nicely. Andy shows up with my mom and dad and comes over and asks if we can talk. He looks so handsome, not dressed for the wedding yet, but he looks fit and has great color in his face. Andy, by anyone's standards, is a very good-looking guy. His dark brown hair is graying a bit, he has the most beautiful brown eyes, and he wears a goatee. He's about five foot eleven, and although still thin for his height, he's filled out and doesn't look sick. But he does look nervous.

"What is it, Andy?" I ask him, my excitement shining through.

"Cass, I'm not sure about this," he says.

"Sure about what?" I respond, hoping he doesn't mean the wedding.

"This whole wedding thing. I mean what's the point?"

"Andy, is this a philosophical conversation you want to have about marriage as a union, and what's the point and necessity of a piece of paper where hearts are concerned? Please tell me that's what this is about and not that you don't want to marry Tracy."

"Cass, I don't think I can do this."

"Andy, don't you think it's kind of late to be getting cold feet? I mean, look around you. Guests, including your intended, will be arriving soon."

He says softly, "It's not cold feet. This isn't fair to Tracy. I don't want her to be a young widow. That has such a stigma attached to it."

Astonished, I reply, "What century do you think we live in? There's no stigma, *and* Tracy is a big girl. She knows what she's getting into, and she knows more than anything she wants to be your wife, for an hour, for a day, for a month, or for years. What is it with you, Elizabeth, and Christy? Do you guys really believe she's going to hurt less if something happens to you because there's no license that says you're married? How shallow do you think she is? She loves you, Andy, with everything she is. She loves you, and you love her just the same, if not more. If you don't marry her today, I will! One way or another, a wedding is happening, with or without you. Now, knock this off and let's get you dressed, OK?"

Andy smiles as if he feels a little silly. "OK, Cass, let's do this."

"That's better. Come on," I say, putting my hand around his arm.

Thirteen

The ceremony was just beautiful. No, it was beyond beautiful, magical. Tracy took everyone's breath away when she walked down the aisle. She looked like the proverbial princess. They wrote their own vows and both struggled to get the words out, their tears and emotions getting in the way. There wasn't a dry eye; you could hear the sobs. The reception was so much fun, the food delicious, the atmosphere filled with love and gratitude. We had live music and danced past midnight. My dad even got up and danced! My evening was topped off when I got a text from Daniel. "Thinking of you on this most auspicious of days. Congratulations to all of you!" I text back, "Wish you could be here, Dan. Everyone is drinking, dancing, and having a great time!" He replies, "One day I will hold you in my arms and dance with you." That makes me smile.

Andy and Tracy head to Europe for twelve days after the ceremony, compliments of my mom and dad. Dr. B gave her blessing for Andy to travel, especially since all his latest scans showed the disease is stable. If anyone needs to be away and have a vacation, it's those two. They started in London, where they spent six days, and they just arrived in Paris to spend the next six. They text regularly and send pictures. They look so happy.

On their second day in Paris, I get a call from Tracy at around two in the morning. I'm immediately concerned. There's no reason she'd be calling at this hour unless something is wrong. "I'm sorry for calling at this hour—" she starts, but I interrupt her.

"Tracy, what's wrong? How's Andy?" I ask frantically, looking over at Steve, who also awoke when the phone rang.

"Not good, Cass. For about two days he's been getting really bad headaches. At first we didn't think much of it, but now he has double vision and is having pain in his back again. The pain pills seem to help with his back but do nothing for his headaches."

I'm confused. All of his tests showed everything to be stable. Dr. B even did an MRI of the brain and spine, and everything looked good. "Listen, Tracy. I'm going to telephone the oncologist on call and get right back to you. Try not to worry. Remember, everything is stable. Maybe he picked up some kind of virus or something."

I hang up and make the call. As always, the doctor on call gets back to me right away. I explain to him Andy's symptoms, and he tells me he wants to talk to Dr. B in the morning to discuss it further and she or her nurse case manager will call me soon after that to see how we should proceed. He also tells me to try not to worry because all his recent tests show everything's looking good. He recommends Andy double up on his pain meds for the time being and for him to try to stay ahead of the pain.

I call Tracy and give her the information. She's so worried. "Cass, I've never seen him like this. We can't even leave the hotel room," she says.

"OK, Tracy, hang in there. We'll figure it out."

I can't sleep for the rest of the night. I'm dying to go to the Internet and look his symptoms up, but anyone with half a brain will tell you not to do that. It only makes you crazier. Steve tries to reassure me that everything must be OK because of the tests. That's the only thing keeping me from becoming completely insane. Andy's so far away, and not being there with him makes me feel so helpless and scared.

The next morning, early, Dr. B calls me and asks me again to describe the symptoms Andy's having. I tell her excruciating headaches, double vision, and pain in his back again. I explain the pain pills do nothing for the headaches. She asks if he's having any problems with his speech. I say Tracy didn't mention that but I'm sure she would have if that were the case.

"Cass, I don't want to alarm you, but I think it might be a good idea if Andy cut his trip short and got back as soon as possible," she says. Whenever a doctor starts a sentence with, "I don't want to alarm you," that's your cue to fasten your seat belt because this nice, peaceful road you think you're on is going to become a collision course, and your world is about to be turned upside down.

Now I'm completely freaked out. "Why? What do you think this is?" I ask her, my fear coming through loud and clear.

She tries to reassure me and says, "I can't speculate without further testing, but I'd like to see him when he returns. In the meantime I'm going to have Elaine make an appointment with our neuro-oncologist."

Neuro-oncologist? OK, now I know this isn't good. That's a brain cancer doctor. "Dr. Babichev, you did an MRI of the brain and everything was fine. Why would he have to see a neurologist?"

She replies, "Again, I don't want to speculate. Let's just get Andy home and take things one step at a time."

I relent and agree, but this is bullshit. Dr. B knows exactly what she thinks this might be. I call Tracy and tell her what Dr. B said. She tells me she's already one step ahead of me because Andy wants to come home right away, and she's currently working on reservations.

"Don't worry about cost, Tracy," I tell her. "Whatever it takes to get on the first flight back, do it."

I pick up Andy and Tracy at the airport the next afternoon, and Andy's in bad shape. It reminds me of when we first started on this road and our first appointment with the first doctor, Dr. Braunstein. Andy is walking with a limp and is thinner than when he left and in so much pain. Tracy got him a patch for his eye to help with the double vision. Man, how quickly things change. One week we're celebrating the beginning of two lives—the next we're facing something possibly catastrophic. Andy isn't the only one who's thinner. Tracy also looks like she needs a meal. Our appointments with Dr. B and the neuro-oncologist, Dr. Maraj, are back to back later that afternoon. We decide to grab a quick bite and head over to the cancer center earlier than the scheduled appointments.

While we're in the reception area, I try to make small talk with Andy and Tracy about their trip and the part of it they were able to enjoy. Andy starts to say something. The words are coherent, but the way he's stringing them together makes no sense at all. I look over at Tracy, and she shrugs her shoulders, looking as confused as I am.

"Andy, what are you saying?" she says. "You aren't making any sense."

At first I think he's joking with us, but he continues to talk in sentences that make no sense at all. What the hell is happening? I ask Tracy if this has been happening. She shakes her head no, her eyes filling with tears.

While we are waiting, I text Dan, "Have I told you lately how much I miss you?"

He texts back, "Not half as much as I miss you. When can I see you?"

I reply, "Soon, I hope."

He responds, "Me too, Cass."

They call us back, and to our surprise both Dr. B and another doctor are there. It's Dr. Maraj. Dr. B introduces us, and before she has a chance to say anything further, I tell them what just happened in the reception area. The doctors exchange a look.

I finally say, "OK, enough. Something is going on, and we need to know what it is. I don't want to wait for tests and all that other stuff. I'll be dead from a heart attack well before then. Please just tell us at least what you think is going on."

Dr. Maraj, a small, bald man with what sounds like an Indian accent, begins to explain. "From what you're describing and considering the type of cancer Andy has, it could be—and please allow me to qualify, we can't know anything for sure until we do further the testing"—*yeah, yeah, yeah,* I think, getting really exasperated with every word he says, *get to the point already*—"we could be looking at cancer that has spread to the fluid in the spine and the lining of the brain."

There's dead silence in the room. I'm waiting for one of them to say, "Don't worry. We have medicines that will treat this and get Andy right back where he was before this," but neither one of them is saying anything.

"What about the MRI of the brain and spine? It showed everything was fine, no tumors," I say with quiet desperation in my voice.

Dr. Maraj continues. "This is much different than typical tumors. These are cells that float around in the fluid that goes up and down the spine, and they find places to hide and lodge, if you will, along the nerves in the spine, which could explain Andy's back pain, and in what we call the meninges of the brain, which could explain the headaches, double vision, and now problems with his speech."

"The what—what are meninges?" I ask, still stunned and confused.

"The lining of the brain," he answers. "I'd like to do another MRI, one that's more sensitive, to see if there's enhancement in the lining and to see if there are any lesions the other MRI didn't pick up. We'll also do a spinal tap to test the fluid in Andy's spine to see if there are cancer cells floating around in there."

I don't even think I want to ask the next question, but I do anyway. "How is this treated?"

"We surgically install what's called an Ommaya reservoir that's like a catheter system. If what we suspect is true, Andy has a buildup of fluid in his brain, and this will help drain that fluid and give him relief from the symptoms he's experiencing. It will also allow us to deliver chemotherapy to the brain and spine through the reservoir."

"So there's a treatment, then?" I ask somewhat optimistically. They give each other that look again. It's like Andy isn't even here; he's in too much pain to give a shit.

"Well, with treatment," Dr. Manaj continues, "which has some harsh side effects, we're looking at about four to six months, and without treatment one to three months. The decline either way is—how do I say—"

I interrupt, saying, "Not pretty?"

"Yes, not pretty. Andy will more than likely lose his ability to speak and walk and have significant memory problems. He may also become incontinent and lose control of his bowels," he says as gently as he can.

Tracy gets up and leaves the room, crying. Holy Jesus, I can't even think of a scenario that's more awful than this.

"In the meantime, while we're doing the testing and waiting for more conclusive results, we can add morphine to Andy's pain management regimen. What you described to us in the reception area sounds like a seizure, which is very common with this type of disease, so I'd like to start him on seizure medication as well."

"What's this type of disease called?" I ask.

"Leptomeningeal carcinomatosis. We'd like to do the spinal tap today and schedule the MRI for sometime this week."

***

A week later we get the results back. It's what they suspected it was, but I already know that. I've been numb, not really allowing myself to feel much of anything. When speaking to my family about this, I'm very matter of fact, not offering an ounce of hope. There is none when things progress to this point. My mom and dad keep calling me, asking the same questions repeatedly, expecting different answers. Andy's scheduled to have the Ommaya reservoir installed next week. The morphine has helped his pain somewhat, so that's good.

Andy calls and asks me to come to his house; he wants to talk to me. When I arrive at his house, Tracy's car is gone. She must be out running errands. She is still working part time. William, Aamina, Allison, and Kyle are at their house quite often. All of our lives are revolving around Andy and trying to soak up what precious time we have left with him. My dad, and even my mom, have completely come out of retirement to run Andy's business. I let myself in, make myself a cup of coffee, and head upstairs to Andy and Tracy's bedroom. He's lying in bed. He looks thinner and thinner every day.

"Hey, Andy, how's it going today?" Ridiculous question.

"Oh, I'm dying. Other than that, fine." He smiles.

"Well, that's good, not the dying part, the fine part," I say jokingly. "You know, this really isn't cool what you're doing, this dying stuff—not cool at all."

He laughs. "Yeah, well, you know, what's a man to do? Cass," he says, changing the subject, "you've got to promise me a couple of things. First, I need to know that you'll always be there for Tracy."

"Of course I will, Andy."

He continues, "If at any point I become—for lack of better words—incompetent or an imbecile, stop treatment. I made you my medical director because I know you will carry out my wishes and not let your emotions get in the way. Tracy is far too emotional and fragile to make these types of decisions."

My eyes fill with tears. "Yes, Andy, I'll stop treatment." I look down and start crying.

"If I start to lose control of my bodily functions, I don't want to be around anymore. Take care of that for me."

What? I look up at him. What's he asking of me? "Andy, what do you mean, 'Take care of that for me'?"

He looks me straight in the eyes and says again, "Take care of that for me."

Now I know what he's asking, but I also know I'd do anything for Andy—anything but that. I change the subject, and through tears I say, "Andy, you have to get better so we can run our favorite snake trail again."

"Cass, you and I both know I won't be doing that run, but one day, after I'm gone, take William and run the snake trail for me." He takes off his black bracelet he's worn for as long as I remember and gives it to me.

"I will, Andy," I say, sobbing as I put the bracelet on. I then bury my head into his chest and cry and cry.

Andy has his arms around me, and he cries as well. "Thanks, Cass, for everything, and please, when the time comes, thank everyone else for me."

"I will, Andy, and thank you for being the best brother and friend anyone could ever ask for. I love you." I can barely get the words out.

"I love you, too, Cass. Want to know a secret?" he asks me.

"Sure," I reply.

"I'm scared…scared of dying," he answers.

"Well, of course you're scared because you've never done it before…at least not that you know of." He laughs. I cry.

Fourteen

$\mathcal{A}$ndy had his surgery for the reservoir. The good news is the pressure and pain he's been feeling in his head is all but gone. The fluid drains down this long tube that runs along the inside of his head, down his neck, and to his abdomen. The double vision is gone as well.

The whole family, with the exception of our kids, is at Andy and Tracy's house one evening shortly after his surgery. He called everyone together to tell them his decision not to undergo any more chemo. The side effects are too brutal, and he's just tired. "What's another month or two if I'm going to be throwing up and sick the whole time?" he says. Tracy and I already knew and agree and respect Andy's decision, but everyone else is surprised. Allison is in too much shock to speak, and William says he respects Andy's decision either way. My parents want him to continue treatment. "You never know, maybe it will reverse things. They told you before you had only four to six months and look at you. You've survived way past that point," my mom says.

"I agree," Allison is finally able to voice.

"This is different, Mom," I break in quietly.

Allison jumps up and angrily says to me, "How is this different? Why are you willing to throw in the towel so easily on your brother?"

"What did you say to me? Throw in the towel?" I say with disgust and bewilderment. Everyone is stunned and dumbfounded by her comment.

"I just mean—well, we can't—we have…" She stutters and stammers her words while we all look at her, still astonished by her hateful words. "We can't give up," she says softly, embarrassed. Sometimes some words can't be taken back once spoken, no matter how many apologies or explanations are offered. This is one of those times.

Andy finally says, "This is my decision to make, and I've made it."

I call Dr. B that night and tell her of Andy's decision to stop treatment. She says she understands and will have Elaine, her nurse case manager, call me so we can arrange hospice care. She explains that everything that happens from this point on is palliative, keeping Andy as comfortable and as pain-free as possible. She also says that once hospice comes in, she's technically out of the picture but we should feel free to call her anytime. I ask her one more time how much time she thinks Andy has without treatment. She says with Andy it's hard to tell—he's surprised her so many times—but considering that he's young and still relatively strong, it could be up to three months.

"Dr. Babichev, I want to thank you, really thank you, for all you've done for Andy and for giving us more time," I say sincerely.

"You're welcome. You're a great sister, Cassandra. We all think so. Andy's lucky to have you."

I'm the lucky one.

*A*ll the arrangements for hospice are in place. A nurse comes once or twice a week, checks Andy's vitals, and makes sure he's as comfortable as he can be. They also offered to have someone come in twice a week to shave Andy and help with bathing, but we decided against it. Tracy and I have that covered. No one else is touching Andy in that way. Yes, I've crossed that boundary. I change him, feed him, bathe him. Andy isn't at all who he was; he's like a small child, a toddler even. I take care of him as I would my child, not my brother. He can't speak, not real words anyway. It's just jumbled-up words that make no sense to anyone, except maybe Joey, who has these full-on conversations with him. She answers like she knows what he's saying; it's so sweet to watch. He has trouble walking without help and recently became incontinent and lost control of his bowels.

The house is always full—friends, neighbors, and of course all of us. Tracy and I work around the clock trying to take care of Andy's needs with as much dignity as possible. My mom—well, everyone—keeps telling me to eat, that I'm getting too thin. Tell me something I don't know. I can't eat, I can't sleep, and I'm running on pure adrenaline. This is taking its toll on everyone. My dad looks like he's aged twenty years in the last six weeks and has developed high blood pressure. We're all tired.

I haven't been to yoga in over seven weeks now. Daniel texts and calls regularly, but I don't reply or answer as much as I used to. I miss him so much but don't have the energy for anything other than taking care of Andy and my kids. One day, while everyone's at Andy and Tracy's, I decide I need some time alone. I tell Steve I'm going up to the house, that I need some time by myself away from all this. He says for me not to worry and to try to take a nap; he'll stay there with the kids until I get back.

When I get home, I make tea and turn on some music, trying to somehow relax. I decide to call Daniel.

"Cass!" he says, sounding so happy to hear from me.

"Sorry I haven't been in touch—"

"Cass," he says, cutting me off, "no need to apologize. I'm just so happy to hear your voice. I miss you," he says sweetly.

"I miss you too."

"How's your brother?" he asks.

"Not good. Not good at all," I respond.

"Sorry, Cass. I'm so very sorry."

"I know you are, thanks. What are you up to today?"

"Not much. Do you want to take a drive up the coast?" he asks.

I'm not sure if he's serious or not. "Really?" I respond.

"Yeah, really. It might be good for you to get away from this for a while."

Could I really do that? I ask myself. Everyone else is with Andy, the nurse was there yesterday, all his vitals look good…maybe I could. I'm excited for the first time in a long time.

"It's a beautiful day, and there's this beach far up the coast but not too far. It's really secluded, where I go when I want to be alone, meditate, or just think. You could meet me there."

"OK, yeah, I'll meet you there, Dan."

"You just made my day." He gives me directions, not your typical directions. Part of it I can put in my navigation system, but the rest is dirt roads and milestones, this tree, that stone.

I'm getting confused and say, "Look, I'll meet you as far as the navigation will take me. Meet me there, and I'll follow you the rest of the way."

"Good thinking," he says, laughing a bit, probably wondering why he didn't think of that. I call Steve and tell him I'm going for a drive up the coast. He says he thinks that's a great idea and promises to call if anything comes up.

I get to where Dan and I agree to meet, and he's already there, leaning on his car, arms folded, hair down. I realize how much I've missed him, and I practically fly out of my car and run toward him. He has a huge smile and catches me in his arms. "God, I've missed you, Cass," he says so warmly.

"I've missed you, too, Dan."

We hold each other tight, and there's that smell I love. There's the strength of his arms that makes me feel like I can float, like I'm light as a feather and can fly. We get back in our cars, and I follow him. As we twist and turn down dusty, secluded roads, I think how I'd have never found this place alone.

We park and walk down a steep hill toward the shore. As we walk along the shoreline, we start talking about the studio he's opening soon. He's found the space and is in the middle of negotiations. He's really excited. His face lights up as he talks about it.

"I'm really happy for you, Dan. I know you've been wanting to do this for a long time."

"Thanks, Cass." He stops walking, faces me, takes my hands, and holds them to his heart. He looks at me adoringly and says, "I wish I could take your pain away. I really do. There isn't a day that goes by I don't think about you and wish I could see you, be there for you. I take that back. There isn't a minute that goes by I don't think about you. I try to shake it off. I mean, how healthy can this be, right?"

I smile and look into his eyes. "I think about you all the time too, Daniel. When I saw you leaning against your car, arms folded, with your hair down—it's the happiest I've been in a long time. I realized just how much I miss you. I can't explain it. I just can't seem to let go of whatever this is. I'm not sure I even want to."

He responds tenderly, "I can't let it go, Cass. I can't let *you* go. There are days I actually get angry with you for walking into the studio and into my life. The first day I saw you, the first day our eyes met, I knew I was in trouble. Then there are days when I can smell you, feel you, even when you aren't with me. Crazy, I know. I've stopped trying to make sense of it."

This is the most open we've ever been about our feelings for each other. He pulls me in close to him. Oddly, for the first time, I find myself not resisting. His body is close to mine. We're forehead to forehead, then cheek to cheek. I can feel and hear his breath flowing, smooth and deep. His scent is intoxicating.

His movements toward me are deliberate and controlled, as if he doesn't want to frighten me off.

I start to run my hands along his chest. I feel my heart race and my body trembling. I can see the want for me in his eyes, and I can feel the need in his touch. Every time the wind blows, the smell of orange blossoms fills the air around us. Gently he sweeps my hair away from my shoulders and begins to slowly shower my neck with soft kisses. I look up to the clear blue sky, the sun shining warmly down on us. I close my eyes and take a long, deep breath; no feeling could possibly compare to this. His breath is still smooth and deep, each kiss intense, each kiss bliss, each kiss spinning me more and more out of control. He moves up and tenderly kisses my cheek, my forehead, and then my other cheek.

My knees feel week, my mind numb, and my heart overflowing with emotions. He stops and gazes thoughtfully and deeply into my eyes, then sensuously cups my face with his hands and moves his lips steadily and cautiously toward mine. My arms wrapped around his waist, I instinctively press his body closer to mine. He responds in kind. Our breath is now in rhythmic unison, our world moving in slow motion. I don't want this moment to end. His lips finally meet mine, soft, tender, sweet.

Suddenly, like a thunderbolt of lightning, reality comes crashing through, a wrecking ball shattering this beautiful, forbidden space between us. Still holding him, I pull my lips away from his and look down. Barely audible I say, "I can't, Dan."

He holds me closer, sweetly kisses my forehead, and replies, "I know, Cass."

Now looking into his eyes, I gently sweep back the hair blowing in his face. I lovingly kiss him and whisper, "Thank you, Daniel, for giving me this moment in time."

As I turn and walk away, I look up to the clear blue sky, sun shining warmly down on me. I close my eyes, take a long, deep breath, and wipe away the tears streaming down my face. No feeling could possibly compare to this.

I get back to Andy and Tracy's around dinnertime. Only the family and Mark are there; all the other people who stop by during these days are very mindful not to overstay their welcome and all are gone by dinner so the family can have their time together. Mark, as far as we're all concerned, is family, so that unwritten rule doesn't apply to him. Allison and my mom have made dinner as usual. They put it out, buffet-style, and announce it's ready. Andy's in his favorite chair, just kind of staring off into space. I wonder what he thinks about, if he even thinks at all. We usually take turns feeding him. My kids, nieces, and nephews all fight over who's next; they really love Uncle Andy, and this is hard on all of them.

As Mark and I make our way around the dinner table, filling our plates, he leans in close to me and whispers, "You were with him, weren't you?"

I look at him, surprised. How could he know that? "What makes you think that?" I ask.

"Oh, maybe the mixed scent of fresh vanilla and sandalwood."

I immediately start sniffing my arms and shirt, almost spilling my food.

"Cass, relax. I'm kidding. I can't smell anything. Since you've been back, every once in a while, you get this faraway look with a smile on your face, and then you gently touch your lips with your fingers."

"Stop it, Mark. You're scaring me!" I whisper.

"I knew it. You *were* with him!"

We go and sit in the living room where we can have some privacy. Everyone else is either outside or in the family room. I tell Mark everything that happened, from the phone call all the way up to the kiss. He takes my plate and his, puts them down on the coffee table in front of us, pulls me in close to him, and says, "Cass, that would be a very, very sweet story if you weren't married with two kids. Oh, dear, what am I going to do with you?"

ay by day, Andy's progressively gotten worse. It's so hard to watch someone you love so much not only deteriorate right before your eyes but also in a way that's so inhumane and humiliating. I understand now more than ever Andy's request to not allow him to go through this, but I'm helpless to do anything. That's not something I could live with. I feel guilty sometimes not being able to honor his wish, but in my heart I know who I am and what I'm capable of, and that's not something I could do.

Our hospice case coordinator calls to tell me the whole team, including their spiritual counselor, will be coming by later that afternoon to check on things. So far we've all declined counseling from hospice, none of us really the type to sit, individually or collectively, discussing our feelings. I guess with Andy getting worse they want to make sure we know it's available.

Tracy is at her mom's taking a much-needed break, and the cousins are out at dinner and then going to a movie. The rest of us are at Andy and Tracy's, Mark as well; he barely leaves my side lately, except when he has to work. The hospice team arrives: the nurse practitioner, the regular nurse who comes twice a week, the administrator we met with in the very beginning, and the spiritual counselor. The nurse goes upstairs and checks on Andy while the administrator sits with the rest of us downstairs and begins to discuss the end-of-life issues we've already touched on. She goes into more detail about the proper protocol that needs to be followed once he does pass. We're all so absolutely exhausted and spent that we're not getting emotional, not even my mom. We're just taking it all in, stone-faced.

The nurse comes down and explains to us that Andy's starting to show signs of end of life. *Really?* I want to say. She also has her own set of special instructions for us. She explains a normal process of dying is a rattle we'll start to hear when Andy breathes. She tells us not to be alarmed and explains it's caused by mucus buildup in the back of the throat. She's talking about the death rattle but doesn't call it that; apparently once you hear it, there's no mistaking it. We're all sitting there staring at the nurse and administrator while they speak, looking uninterested, but really we just have nothing left.

Then the spiritual counselor starts in. "Feel free to feel the feelings you feel. Try not to judge yourself and each other. Grief affects us all in different ways, and we all grieve differently. Try to have compassion for yourself, allowing yourself to go through this rainbow of emotions you'll be having."

Did he just say "rainbow of emotions"? I don't know why that strikes me as funny. I just don't put a rainbow to anything I've been feeling. Rainbows conjure up images of butterflies and lilies in a field after a fresh spring rain. It sounds like *Mr. Roger's Neighborhood* or the *Land of Oz*, not the hellish devil's inferno this damned cancer has been putting us through.

I put my head down and start to laugh, quietly at first. "That's good, Cassandra," he says. "Feel what you're feeling." I start to laugh harder, my head still down, my shoulders shaking up and down with my hand covering my face so he can't see it's laughter. Mark knows, though, and now his head is down in his hand. "That's good, very good," the counselor continues. "Everyone just go with it. Don't resist."

The counselor continues consoling us, thinking he's making some major headway. Steve is next—his head goes down—then William, then my dad. Anyone who knows me knows I'm laughing, not crying. Allison, my mom, and Kyle are keeping their composure and nodding their heads in agreement with the counselor. Appearances, don't you know? Mark, Steve, William, my dad, and I are all laughing now, heads down, hands on our faces. How rude are we? We can't help it, though. I think it's combination of no sleep, heartache, and this clown who looks like he's mere seconds out of the womb thinking he can counsel this group of cynical, slightly arrogant, barely there intellectuals who, combined, have more life experience then he'll ever have in several lifetimes.

I excuse myself and walk out. "It's OK, Cassandra. Feel. Feel," he says as I leave.

Steve and Mark are next, telling him they need to check on me. William and my dad aren't far behind. We go outside, and there's no mistaking the bellows of laughter coming from the front of the house. As the laughter slows, Steve and I look at each other. We haven't laughed like that together in a very long time. The way he looks at me is something I haven't seen in a long time either. It's a want, a desire, a look of love that's been missing in our relationship for far too long. I walk over to Steve, put my arm around his arm, and tell Mark, William, and my dad that me and my man have some unfinished business to take care of. They smile, and I can't believe I just said that in front of my father.

We get into Steve's car and drive home. We practically rip each other's clothes off before even getting in the door. We make our way upstairs to the bedroom.

"God, I've missed you, Cass. I've missed this. I've missed us." He's looking at me so lovingly, so wantingly.

I reach my hand up to his neck and pull him toward me. I kiss him like it's our first time. We are holding on to more than each other; we are holding on to this moment, these feelings, not wanting it to slip away from us again. He has his head buried in my neck as he enters me slowly, taking his time, and my hands are on his lower back, encouraging him in deeper. He starts kissing me again with vigor, every movement, every thrust inspired and enhanced by our emotions. We make love so passionately and so completely that I tear up as I climax.

"Wow," I say to Steve. "Where did that come from?"

"I love you, Cass. I love you."

"That, Steve, is the depth I was talking about."

He holds me, and we fall asleep in each other's arms.

Fifteen

With the exception of my mom and dad, we've all been sleeping at Andy and Tracy's for the past three nights. Clearly the end is very near. He doesn't eat at all and drinks very little. I give him little pieces of ice chips to moisten his mouth, but even the little I give him he sometimes chokes on. He's on morphine every hour to help his breathing, which has become very labored.

Mark and William help me get Andy into the tub for his evening bath; he can't stand anymore but can still sit up, so we've gone from showers to baths. I close the door—I don't like anyone seeing Andy in this vulnerable state. Tracy and I are the only ones who take care of changing his diapers—they can give them any adult name they want, but they're still diapers—and bathing him. I start to bathe Andy. He loves the water; he always seems very content and peaceful during his bath.

"You know, Andy," I say, "I was reading somewhere that if you tell your loved one that it's OK for them to go, they may actually go. Well, I want you to know it's OK. I've got this. I'll take care of Tracy, Mom, Dad, all your nieces and nephews, everyone. So, yeah, you can go now. I know you feel you have to fight and hang on, but letting go is sometimes the strong thing to do. I know this, you see, but in a very different way than you might have ever imagined. There's this guy—his name is Daniel. I've known him for about three years. I've mentioned him to you but only as someone I take yoga with. I couldn't ever tell you the real story because, Andy—let's face it—I love you, but sometimes you can be very righteous about things. No, no, don't try to argue. You know you can." Andy's just staring off into space, playing with the soap bar.

"Anytime I thought about telling you, I'd chicken out because I hate it when you're disappointed in me. I'm not going to get into all the psychological underpinnings of how or why I let something like this happen, almost blowing years and years of marriage and splitting my family apart. That would reduce it—and me—down to something very mediocre, and I'd rather live with the fantasy that somehow Daniel and I were different. I'd like to say it wasn't an affair, but anything you can't do in front of your spouse kind of falls into that arena, right? Maybe, I don't know for sure. We did share some really tender moments and were sort of intimate—not really intimate, because intimate usually suggests something sexual. It was kind of sexual, but only because of the physiological response it triggered. OK, forget it. The point is, Steve and I seem to be getting back on track in our marriage. Things aren't perfect, but we're getting better. Daniel's been trying to get in touch, but I haven't texted or called him back.

"I'd be lying if I said I don't want to because I do. I really, really do. I miss him. That missing feels like an ache inside. I know it's for the best because—maybe I forgot to mention—he's also married with two kids. I know; I know. What the hell was I thinking? That's just it; I wasn't thinking. I was feeling without thinking. Thinking and feeling are good; feeling without thinking can get you into trouble. You'll be happy to know that it's over now. I'm committed to making things work with Steve. I've thought quite a bit about the karmic ramifications of all of this. I know you don't necessarily subscribe to all that karmic action stuff, but you know I do. The way I view it, seeing my brother naked, changing his diapers, and having to bathe and clean, well, you know, certain areas—karmically what I did with Daniel and what I'm doing here with you, they kind of cancel each other out. So I break even—don't you think? So, there it is; I finally told you. You're free to go now, Andy. Be free, my sweet brother. Be free." I call William and Mark to help me get Andy out of the tub and dressed.

Two days later Andy checks out. He's not here anymore. His body is still here, but he isn't. He no longer grips my hand when I hold his. His breathing is very heavy, with that awful sound the nurse was telling us about. You definitely do know the death rattle when you hear it; it's beyond horrible. He just lies there motionless, fighting for every breath. I don't think it's him fighting; I think it's his body trying to find the off switch. The hospice nurse says it's OK to increase his doses of morphine. He's lying on his side in bed, and I'm spooning him. Tracy is on the other side, usually with her head resting on his. The only time we get up is to use the restroom. He's damp and cold to the touch. His body has what looks like purple and blue splotches on it, especially on his arms and legs. If I pick up his arm, it just falls right back down. Yes, Andy's soul has left the building.

That night we're all camped out in Andy's room, sleeping bags everywhere. Andy's surrounded by everyone he loves and everyone who loves him. The cousins are all there, the older ones caring and supporting the younger ones. It's such a beautiful scene. I'm still next to Andy, holding him tight, smelling him, missing him. My mom and dad are completely heartbroken. We all are. I continue to give Andy morphine every hour.

At around four in the morning, I notice his breathing calming, and intuitively I know he doesn't have many breaths left. I quietly wake up William, Steve, Allison, Tracy, and Mark.

Everyone else is still sleeping. I stand beside Andy's bed with my hand on his shoulder, the six of us in a semicircle around Andy's bed. We're all silently watching him. We glance at each other every once in a while with looks of love and support. Finally, Andy looks up to the ceiling, takes a long inhale, exhales slightly, and that's it. He's gone. It's so beautiful, like a baby bird struggling to take its first breath. Andy looked just like that little bird, only taking his last.

We wake everyone up. We don't even have to say anything. Everyone knows and gathers around his bed. The sound of silent sobs fills the room. We all just stare at Andy with a mixture of relief, sadness, disbelief, and most of all, love. Whoever says you can't hear hearts breaking has never experienced the loss of someone close to them. It's the loudest and most profound sound you'll ever hear. It's odd, but I can't cry. I just walk over to my kids, nieces, nephews, to everyone and smile and hold them each for a moment or two. My mom sits at Andy's side, sobbing uncontrollably with her head buried in his chest. Tracy's next to him on the other side, silently crying and quietly calling out his name. My dad sits in a chair with his head down, crying.

About an hour later, I call hospice and tell them Andy's passed away. They call the crematorium we've chosen and inform them so they can send someone over to pick up his body. I go to his closet and pick out a pair of jeans and a shirt for him to wear and his favorite sneakers. I take them to Tracy for her approval. She nods and cries even harder. All of his nieces and nephews write letters to Andy that we'll put in his pants pocket.

A two-man team arrives from the crematorium an hour and a half later; they're very professional and sensitive of this process. Since I have medical directive, they hand me the paperwork to fill out and sign. They also tell me that sometimes removal of the body is too much for some family members and that maybe some should leave the area until he's put in the van. I tell my older nephews and nieces to take the younger ones into the family room. They all say their final good-byes, each kissing him and giving him one final touch. The rest of us decide to stay with Andy until he's put in the van. I can't even imagine leaving him alone. I still can't cry. I guess I'm either too busy taking care of business and everyone around me or afraid of my own emotions. I give one of the men Andy's clothes, which they'll put on him before they cremate him. I wonder if they actually do that or if they just let the families think they do. Either way, I guess, it makes no difference; this isn't Andy anymore anyway. They zip him up in a big white bag—*Better than black*, I think—put him on a gurney, and take him downstairs.

My mom goes from subdued crying to an out-of-control frenzy. She starts yelling as they take him away, "No, no, no. Don't take him. Andy, Andy, Andy! My baby, my baby. He's gone. He's gone!"

Allison and Kyle try to console her the best they can. As the men get Andy to the front door, I ask them to stop. I haven't said my good-bye yet. I ask the man to please unzip the bag for a moment. He compassionately nods his head and says for me to take my time. Andy's arms are folded across his chest, and his eyes are now closed, his mouth slightly open. He looks like he's sleeping soundly. I lean down and kiss his forehead as I touch his hands. I whisper in his ear, "You're free now, Andy. Stop by every once in a while and let me know you're all right. Always remember me, and please watch over Joey and Lance." My eyes fill with tears as I give him one last kiss and tell him I love him.

⌒

The next morning I wake up, and for a split second, I think everything is OK. Then I remember what's happened. I look at the center of my bed and see a gigantic hole. I'm lying at the edge of an abyss, almost falling in. I try to yell for Steve, but, "No, no, no!" is all I can say. I keep yelling over and over again. "No, no, no!" Steve comes running in. I tell him to call Allison and William to cancel the memorial. "No memorial," I tell him. "Too soon, too soon." I'm overwrought at this point. Steve just holds me tighter and tighter. "No, let go of me!" I yell. "Call them. Call them. No memorial!" I yell even louder. "Call them, dammit, no memorial. I have to go to Andy's; I have to take care of Andy! That's what I do every morning. What am I going to do this morning? What am I going to do this morning?"

I'm talking crazy now; I can't even think straight. I never imagined something could hurt this bad. Steve keeps trying to calm me down and hold me. For some reason I get up and start to clean, frantically clean. Steve follows me around the house, still trying to calm me. The kids are fortunately so wiped out they're sleeping very soundly. Steve shuts their doors. "Cass, come here, baby. Just sit here with me. You can clean later."

I look at him like he's the crazy one. "No, I have to clean now. Everything has to be clean. Cancel the memorial, no memorial."

"OK, baby, no memorial. I'll call them. No memorial."

I'm relieved now, no memorial. There's an emptiness inside that quickly fills itself with pain and sorrow, so I'm not empty anymore. I'm full, really full. I wonder how anyone gets through this type of pain. Do people truly make it to the other side of this? This is beyond pain. It's like belly flopping every thirty seconds onto a bed of needles. Every part of me hurts. Life is now without Andy. How can that be? How is that even possible? I walk upstairs and into my closet, but I don't know what I'm doing once I get there. I lie on the floor in the fetal position. Steve comes in and spoons me as I rock back and forth, my arms clenching my stomach. I quietly keep calling out, "Andy, Andy, Andy." *I can't do this,* I keep thinking. *I can't get through this.* It doesn't seem humanly possible that one can endure this kind of agony and survive.

I pass the baton to William and Allison; they're making all the arrangements for the memorial that's scheduled for the following weekend. I really only have two things left to do: take care of the cremation—pick up his ashes—and give a speech at his memorial. Beyond that I can't do one more thing. I've done all I can for Andy.

The day before the memorial my mom takes my dad to the emergency room with really bad chest pains. He's admitted to the intensive care unit and is diagnosed with a tear in the aorta. Since Andy was diagnosed with cancer, he just stopped taking care of himself. What's happening to him now has been a few years in the making. You can't let yourself go like that without some major repercussions, especially in your eighties, but talk about getting hit twice and hard. First Andy, then my dad. Is the universe playing some kind of sick joke on us? My dad obviously can't attend the memorial, and even if this didn't happen to him, I don't think he could've handled it anyway. He's a broken man, plain and simple.

⟵⟶

The memorial is just beautiful. Allison and William did a wonderful job. There are around three hundred people in attendance. Andy was very loved in the communities he worked and lived in. Steve would have to hire movie extras for my memorial to get even a quarter of this number. It's standing room only.

William and his son, the eldest of the cousins, speak, as does Andy's best friend. The cousins made a video montage that we play to some of Andy's favorite music. We have a big picture of Andy in the center of the room with gorgeous flowers arranged all around it. When it's my turn to speak, I'm not sure I can do it. I don't like to show my emotions in front of people outside of my little circle and certainly do not like to be the focus of all this attention. I know this is something I have to do for Andy. I get up and have to sit back down.

Steve says, "Come on, Cass. I'll walk you to the podium. You can do this." I compose myself and take long, deep breaths as

Steve walks me up. My heart's racing, and for some reason only the left side of my body is shaking.

As I stand up there, I start slowly looking around the room, starting with all the people on the left, then the center, followed by the right and back around again. It's truly amazing, all these people here for Andy. I calm down but still can't speak yet. I keep looking at all the people, staring into their eyes as they look back at me, waiting for me to say something. The room is so silent you could hear a pin drop. Steve is standing by the wall behind me, so I can't see him, but I look to where William and Mark are sitting. They both nod their heads, letting me know it's going to be all right.

I begin, saying, "On January sixteenth, 1964, at seven twenty in the morning, Stuart and Beth Stevens gave birth to a beautiful baby, a son. They named him Andrew Charles, Andrew Charles Stevens. Through the years he also became known as Andy, Uncle A, Aceman, and Drew. What Stuart and Beth couldn't have known is that they gave birth to more than just a boy, a son. They gave the world a blessed gift. They gave us a boy who would grow up to be a man who was so pure, so gentle, so kind, and so very loyal. Andy always saw the best in everyone and always brought out the best in all of us. He taught us the true meaning of compassion, forgiveness, and unconditional love.

"Foremost, I'd like to thank my mom and dad for raising such a fine man and for giving us a brother, an uncle, a husband, and a friend. His humor, his wit, and his laughter will be missed by all of us. His strength and courage will endure and will be part of his legacy that lives in each one of us. My father, our patriarch, who can't be with us here today, is our leader and our guide. He's taught us patience and acceptance; it's no wonder Andy was who he was. Mom, you've taught us dignity and grace in the face of adversity. Allison and Kyle, you've always stood steadfastly by the family at all costs. William, my brother and my mentor, I trust in you, and I love you. I know you'll guide this family with the same fortitude and pride that our father and Andy have set forth. Aamina, my sister-in-law and my friend, we've learned from you what good mothers do, what good friends do, and your love for Andy will live on and on. Mark, my best friend and my rock, I think I'm slowly getting over the fact that you got more smiles from Andy toward the end of his life than I did. You two shared a very special relationship, and he loved you so much. Steve, my husband, what did I do to deserve a man like you? Andy never let a conversation go by without reminding me of what a true gentlemen you are and how lucky I am to have you. My babies, Joey and Lance, what can I say? You let your mommy do whatever she had to do to be with her brother. You're both mature beyond your years. You stood by me, by your cousins, by Aunt Tracy, and by your Uncle Andy. You're our angels.

"Family was the most important thing to Andy. He had many passions, from golf to running, from tending to his garden to chasing rabbits out of his yard to his love of music. His greatest passion of all, however, was his family and his friends, and most of all, his beloved high school sweetheart, Tracy, who stood tirelessly by his side, fighting every step of the way and never giving up hope. In the last months of his life, it was around-the-clock care. She juiced, she cooked nutritious meals, she cleaned, but most of all she loved. She showed Andy a kind of love usually reserved for the storybooks. She fought hard for not only her husband but for her soul mate, the man she was meant to be with. Tracy, through this experience we've formed an unbreakable bond. The ups, the downs, the laughter, the tears, the pain, the joy, the frustrations, and the triumphs—we've shared them all. I love you dearly and will always be there for you, just as I know you'll always be there for me.

"Uncle Andy—or Uncle A as he was called by most of them— lives in the hearts of the many nieces and nephews he leaves behind. In many of our conversations he'd stop, no matter the topic, and say, 'Cass, man, we're lucky. Look at your kids and our nieces and nephews. From the oldest all the way to the youngest, they're great kids, aren't they?' Yes, Andy, they're great kids, compassionate, loving, and caring, just as you were. There are so many moments toward the end, too many to mention, of his nieces and nephews by his side, taking care of him. He was proud. We're proud.

"A few months before he passed away, he had me over to his house, and we talked about many things that day. I told him he needed to get better so we could run our favorite trail; we called it the snake trail. He said in a very matter-of-fact way, 'Cass, you and I both know I won't be doing that run, but do me a favor. After I'm gone take William and run it for me. Do me another favor, when the time comes; thank everyone for all they've done.' So, the time has come, and on behalf of Andy, my brother, my best friend, thank you."

I somehow get through it without breaking down. Everyone claps, and some even begin to shout, "Andy! Andy! Andy!" I pause and, smiling, slowly take one final look around the room. *That's it, Andy. We're done here*, I say to myself. *We did it.*

At the end of the memorial, all the family, including Mark, stand in the receiving line. I don't cry, even though I feel some people, when they come up to give their condolences, really want me to. I still can't get over how many people are here, some I don't know and many I do, some I haven't seen in years. There are even a few people who came from the health food store where I shop and some friends from yoga. As I'm looking down the line, I'm shocked to see Daniel and Cheryl. As he approaches I feel myself getting anxious. I haven't returned any of his calls or texts and haven't seen him since that fateful day at the beach. Cheryl is first, giving me a hug and telling me how very sorry she is, then Daniel. He comes in toward me, and there's that familiar scent of fresh vanilla and sandalwood that I love so much. He gives me a hug, presses his cheek against mine, and whispers, "I'm still here for you always."

I smile and quietly reply, "Thank you," and he continues down the line.

Mark's right next to me and whispers, "That's him, isn't it?"

I answer, "Yes, that's him."

He gives me a gentle squeeze on my shoulder with a loving smile.

Sixteen

$\mathcal{M}$y father never made it out of the intensive care unit. He passed away almost a month after Andy. His aorta gave way and ruptured, and there was nothing they could do. Looking back on it now, I realize my dad had been dying a slow death since Andy was diagnosed with cancer. Before that, he took care of himself, exercised regularly, and ate healthy. He waited just long enough for Andy to pass and then decided it was his time as well. The doctors can call it what they want; my father died of a broken heart.

My main concern is getting my kids through all of this with as much grace and dignity as possible. They've lost, in a very short time, two very important figures in their lives. It's up to Steve and me to give them the skills they need to deal with these matters of fact. That may sound clinical and sterile, but in my opinion, it's necessary so they can move forward with their lives in a way that's productive and healthy. That doesn't mean we don't show our emotions. We do. I have no problem crying in front of my children, but I get out of bed every morning and do everything I've always done for them: lunches, laundry, shopping, school events, lessons, dinner. I keep their daily routine, especially since these past months have been anything but routine. I still emphasize to them when they walk out the door not to wear their hearts on their sleeves, that there's never an excuse for bad behavior, to do their best, and home is their soft place to land.

Three weeks later I take the kids with me to the crematorium to pick up Andy's ashes. I tell them to wait in the car; I won't be long. I sign all the final paperwork and come out a few minutes later carrying the box containing the beautiful urn William picked out. I'm surprised by how heavy it is. I don't know why; I guess I've just never picked up anyone's ashes before. I walk back to the car and open the trunk and start to put the box there, and then I stop. That doesn't feel right, putting him in the trunk. I open the back door opposite of where Lance's sitting and start to put it there, but that doesn't feel right either. I go to the front passenger side where Joey's sitting and tell her to lift her feet up. I put the box with the ashes there. Yes, that feels right.

I get in and start the car. I look over at Joey sitting there with her feet up, crisscrossed, in the passenger-side seat. L is leaning up between the two front seats, both of them looking at this box. No one says anything, the three of us now, just staring at this box.

Joey finally says slowly and pensively, looking down at the box of Andy's ashes, "Well…this is awkward. Not quite sure what to say at this moment. Umm, welcome back."

L starts to laugh out loud and then catches himself and covers his mouth, thinking he's being disrespectful. I start laughing, then the three of us all laugh together, and it feels so wonderful. I realize they're going to be fine, just fine. My kids are going to be stronger, better people, and I couldn't be more proud of them.

⌒

About six weeks after my dad's passing, we have a memorial of sorts for him. It took six weeks because we wanted everyone there, especially my nieces and nephews, some of whom work and study out of state. It's a small affair with only close friends and family. We have it at his favorite Thai restaurant and bring with us several of bottles of his best wine from his cellar. Before he died he made it clear that's what he wanted us to do. With wine and sake flowing, we're all, surprisingly, having a really good time, talking, laughing, and sharing our favorite memories of my dad and Andy.

As I look around the table filled with family and friends, I think how this is what it's all about, just like that 5K Andy ran when everyone came together and united around him, congratulating him. Yes, we have our differences, but it's the common denominator that we must never lose sight of that keeps the bonds of family and friendship strong. It doesn't mean we are always going to agree or even like each other. It just means when all seems to be going south we unite, are strong, and are there for each other. We all have our quirks and oftentimes dispositions that are hard to understand and accept. We are family, we are friends—perfect, no, but there for each other when it matters most, yes.

I pull Mark aside and say to him, "I don't have the words to thank you, not only for every year I've known you but for these past few years. I couldn't have done it without you, Mark. I mean that."

Mark replies, "Cass, we've been there for each other. Who picked me up off the floor when my mom died? Who held me when I was in the fetal position crying over Greg? Who was there for me when my sweet dog Chi Chi died? And so many other times, too many to mention. You were there without judgment and just loved me."

"Mark, what you did, especially this past year with Andy, was above and beyond—"

He interrupts me by putting his index finger to his lips and whispering, "Shh, Cass, true friendship doesn't know an above and beyond. It only knows here and now and always."

I give him a big hug and kiss. "I love you, Mark."

"I love you more, Cass."

*L*ater that evening I email William:
So, after leaving the memorial for Dad, I realized some-thing profound, maybe only profound to me. I realized that grief and mourning are very solo events. Even though a person may have an infinite amount of support and love around them, like we did tonight, the actual griev-ing process is so personal and so intimate it can't possibly be shared. Maybe because there are no words to describe the depth of emotions, the depth of despair, the depth of the pain, rather than try, we withdraw within and just feel without words, without explanation, without apologies, and without editing. Any expression of it falls short and does Andy, Dad, and us an injustice. I think it's in our si-lence that we can best express our love, our pain, and our loss. The other day I drove to the snake trail and just sat, no tears. Yes, I have the occasional surge of emotions, but they're short-lived, and I shut them down quickly. I don't know where I'll be or what will be the trigger, but the kill shot is on its way, no doubt about it. I guess numb is good right now, "comfortably numb," like the song goes. For how long, who knows? Who cares, really? The absurdity of this isn't lost on me or you. Love you, Cassandra
He emailed me back:
I wish I had something really wise to say but feel the same way. When I'm distracted it's all OK, and then I see their picture or think of them, and I start crying. When numb is the preferred state, that's definitely absurd. Love you too, William

Seventeen

After a long hiatus from my yoga practice, that moment on the beach with Daniel, and the deaths of my brother and father, I start falling deeper and deeper into depression. It takes everything I have to get through the day. Every time I go out, something reminds me of Andy or my dad; it could be anything, like a song on the radio, driving past a golf course, flower fields, orange trees, the grocery store. If I see the same color, make, and model of the cars they used to drive, I rubberneck to see if it's somehow them. Many times I pull over and cry; the pain is just too much to handle. That's why I don't leave the house unless it is absolutely necessary. Too many memories out there lurking, waiting to pounce on my heart and soul when I least suspect it. I'm depressed, I know it, but I hide it well. Mark sees it though and tries to convince me to go back to yoga. He says he's really worried about me mentally and physically.

"Think about your kids, Cass. Think about Steve and your future."

I respond defensively. "What are you saying? I'm fine, the kids are fine, Steve is fine, we're all fine. Are you implying I'm not taking care of my family? I take good care of my family, Mark."

"Cass, you exist; you don't live. You're practically a recluse. You rarely leave the house unless it has something to do with the kids or grocery shopping. Look at you. How much do you weigh? You're probably, what, ninety pounds? You're like a functioning alcoholic, only a functioning depressive. Maybe you've got everyone else fooled with this charade you have going on, but not me."

"Shut up, Mark. Shut up. Just leave it alone! Besides, that's not how this grief stuff works; you don't just wake up one morning and decide you're going to be fine. Grief doesn't care about children, family, age, future. Grief doesn't care how much money you have or don't have, how nice or how mean you are, how good or how bad you are. Grief doesn't discriminate; it's an equal-opportunity destroyer. It just drags you down to your knees as you beg it for mercy from the agony that's ripping you apart from the inside out. At that point you'd be willing to make a deal with the devil for a single moment of relief from the stranglehold it has around your neck, making it so you can't breathe, hear, or see. That's despair. That's darkness. That, Mark, is grief, and you think a yoga class is going to help? Now just leave it and leave me alone!"

"Bullshit, Cass. And I won't leave it alone. I'm not going to sit here and watch my best friend kill herself. You aren't your father, Cass. Don't make the same choices."

That strikes a chord with me. *I'm doing what my father did.*

"Cass, listen," he continues, "I'll give up my own Ashtanga practice and go with you every day to that inferno of a studio for however long it takes, if you just give me one month back on the mat. One month, that's all I ask. Then if you want to go back to your Howard Hughes lifestyle, I'll leave you alone. One month, Cass. One month," he pleads, holding my hands.

Mark thinks if he can get me to class, there'd be no turning back. Yoga truly does get into your cells, and once you've been practicing long enough, that feeling of being drawn in like an addict to crack completely overpowers you. I give in and agree with Mark. I tell him I'll give him his one month, but then he has to get off my back.

By the time I start going back to yoga, Daniel has opened a second studio and is spending more time there than at the original studio. I guess I could go to a different studio, but I think somewhere in my heart I want to see him again. Even just practicing in a studio where he has been satisfies me. I know I still have feelings for him, so avoiding him is best for now. My hope is that these feelings will somehow transform into something that is healthy, and when and if I do see him, we can at least try to be friends. His feelings toward me may have already changed. So for now it's perfect.

Mark and I find our place in a wickedly hot part of the room and practice together almost every day. Day by day, being out of the house and doing something just for me, helps me get through the day. The yoga has been so healing and therapeutic. If there is a day that I am particularly down, I force myself to go, and by the time class is done, I feel stronger and happier. There have been days I have done two classes in the same day. I am starting to put the weight back on that I lost, and food actually tastes good again. I could've never imagined a life without Andy and still it's hard to believe, but there is life after Andy and my dad. There isn't a day that passes when something funny or interesting happens that I don't grab my phone to call Andy to tell him about it, then realize there is no Andy to call. The same with my dad. I took down all the pictures of them. I am not at the point where I can look at them without feeling an incredible amount of pain. Maybe someday I will put their pictures out again, but for now I have to do what gives me the most strength. Mark was right about the yoga. I'm hooked and stronger than before.

Even after two months of being back at yoga, I haven't seen Daniel once. The studio has updated its website, and I can see exactly when he's teaching and where. The days he teaches at the original studio, we either don't go at that time or we go to the new studio. One night after a few too many glasses of wine over dinner with friends, Mark and I sit on the couch in my living room and open another bottle of wine. Everyone else has left, and Steve and the kids have already gone to bed. Steve has been very supportive, and we are really trying to communicate better. He still works long hours, and I find myself missing him and feeling lonely at times. I never bring up Jennifer; dealing with the deaths of Andy and my dad is hard enough. She still works for him. I don't think I am ready to hear about what really happened between them.

Mark pours us more wine and says, "Look, Cass, all this schedule, studio, and class dodging you're doing, trying to avoid Daniel, is getting ridiculous. It's only a matter of time before you run into him. I'm surprised it hasn't happened already. You might as well have it happen on your terms instead of being caught off guard."

He reaches for my laptop to see when Daniel's teaching next, and I beat him to it and tell him, "Tomorrow, ten a.m."

"Tomorrow it is then, you and me together. Look, Cass, you're different now, stronger, better, happier than I've seen you in a long time. You can do this. Whatever it was between you two is in the past, dead, gone."

Confidently I say, "Hell yes, I can do this! I'm stronger, better, happier. He's probably completely forgotten about me anyway."

I commit to going to the 10:00 a.m. class with Mark. I can't help but wonder if somehow the rumors going around the studio about Mark and me—that we're sleeping together—have gotten back to Daniel. We both find the rumor quite entertaining and have done nothing to quiet the gossip. I guess even if the gossip did get back to Daniel, he couldn't care less. I haven't heard from him in quite a while, and I'm pretty certain he's over whatever it was that we shared.

*M*ark and I walk into the 10:00 a.m. class, and there's Daniel behind the counter. He looks up and does a double take. Mark's right behind me. I say, "Hi, Daniel."

He looks down again, shuffling some papers around. He doesn't even look at me, just flatly replies, "Hi."

Mark reaches out his hand to shake Daniel's and says, "I don't think we've ever met. I'm Mark."

Daniel looks up and staring coldly at him, hesitates at first, then finally extends his hand and says, "Daniel. Nice to meet you."

As we walk into the yoga room, I ask Mark, "Were those daggers shooting out from his eyes coming at you or just naked male insecurity?"

Mark, chuckling, says, "I couldn't tell exactly, but pretty sure they were daggers!"

"What *was* that?" I exclaim.

Mark sarcastically replies, "That, my dear, was the iceberg the *Titanic* ran into. They had it flown in for this very occasion."

"Wow," I say, surprised. "I wasn't sure what to expect, but that—that was cold!"

Mark reassuringly says, "Shake it off, Cass. He's just hurt and probably still licking his wounds."

"Well, I can't really blame him after blowing him off the way I did, not returning his texts or calls."

Mark, defending me, says, "Don't go blaming yourself. That's his shit, not yours. Let's have a great class and do what we do best, burn this baby up on our mat!" I lean over, give him a kiss, and thank him for being the best friend a girl could ever have.

During class it's like I'm not there; Daniel avoids my side of the room completely. When we leave, I thank Daniel for class, and, again not looking up, he just says, "Right."

*O*n the drive home, I'm quiet, and Mark asks, "You OK, Cass?"

Quietly I reply, "Yeah, I'll be fine."

"You know, after everything you've told me about him and everything I know about you, I get the attraction that was between you two. I really get it." He gently squeezes my hand and says, "It'll be OK, Cass."

I squeeze his hand back and say, "I know."

He drops me off at home; before going in, I sit outside on a patio chair. My eyes fill with tears, and I'm having a hard time understanding why I feel so much sadness.

*M*ark calls the next day to see how I'm doing. I announce to him that I'm going to Daniel's six-thirty class on Tuesday. I hear him crunching on what sounds like an apple or carrot and ask him to stop; the sound is irritating.

"Will you come with me?" I ask.

"Can't," he replies. "I have a date."

"A date? With who?" I ask.

"Saturday class, second row back, close to the middle, short blond hair, six-pack abs, kinda preppy looking," he answers.

"When did this happen?" I ask, surprised.

"When you were in the changing room."

"Wow, you work fast!" I say, laughing a bit.

"Yeah, we were exchanging glances in class. I'll let you know how it goes." Then he asks, confused, "Why do you want to put yourself through that again?"

"I have no idea, but it's just something I feel I need to do."

Concerned, he states, "Be careful, Cass. You've been through so much, and you have come so far in these past few months. Maybe it wasn't a good idea for you to go to his class. I shouldn't have talked you into it."

"You didn't talk me into it, Mark. I went because I wanted to go."

"OK," he says, "just go with no expectations and wear a winter coat to protect yourself from the cold!" We both laugh.

"Good luck with your date," I tell him.

"Good luck with your class!" he exclaims.

⌒

I walk into Daniel's six-thirty Tuesday evening class. I sign in without so much as saying hello.

"Hey, how are you?" Daniel asks.

Looking down, I curtly reply, "Fine."

"That's it?" he asks.

"That's it," I say, sounding bored.

"Wow!" he says with surprise in his voice.

Quietly so no one around can hear, I tilt my head to one side and snidely remark, "So, Daniel, how does it feel to be on the other side of the chill?"

"So, that's what this is?" he questions.

"Yup, that's what this is," I say indifferently. I walk in and place my mat down next to one of the heaters in my favorite corner. Daniel walks in, pretends to fumble with the heater, and says, "We should talk."

I reply coldly, "No, but we *could* talk."

"Is there a difference?" he asks, clearly irritated.

"Huge," I say nonchalantly.

"When?" he asks.

"When what?" I ask back.

Exasperated, he says, "*Could* we talk?"

"I don't know," I softly respond.

"Soon?" he asks, almost pleading. I just stare at him with a look of disappointment on my face. Still whispering, he asks firmly, "Don't you think you owe me an explanation, something?"

Sternly I reply, "No!"

He says, louder than he wants to, "Come on, no *what?*"

I move in closer. "I owe you nothing, but we could talk," I say, giving in a bit.

He's finally making some headway. He says, "OK, when?"

"I don't know yet," I respond.

With sheer frustration, he says, "You know where to find me," and walks away.

Class begins. He has such command of the room. There are some teachers who, whether you're a beginner, experienced, or somewhere in between, inspire you to do your best. Daniel's one of those teachers. When he gives instruction to the class, it feels like he's speaking to you personally. At least that's how I feel. Right away I notice his attitude is different toward me.

"Beautiful, Cassandra. Arms back even more; you got it... Wow, Cassandra, excellent form. Heels up just a little higher. There it is. Good."

Oh no, I think, *he's doing it again.* He walks by me and confidently gives me that grin. My stomach does a flip just like it used to do. He's paying particular attention to me. "Bring your left hip down, Cassandra, and kick your leg back and up. Try to straighten your leg; you're almost there." I'm completely thrown by the way he's acting toward me, especially considering our interaction before class. I was expecting him to be cool and aloof. *What's his game?* I wonder.

He gets us set up for Triangle, and I see him coming toward me. My heart starts to beat faster. He comes up from behind me and gets into Triangle halfway, his body literally inches from mine. He touches my left hand and gently stretches it up toward the ceiling. "Here, Cassandra," he says softly, "stretch up even more. Good." Then he glides his hand down my arm and brings it to the front of my left shoulder, his fingertips slightly brushing the top of my breast. Using his full palm, he pulls and says, "Shoulder back toward me, Cassandra, bringing both your shoulders in line. There you go." He's speaking softly, sensuously. He then takes his right hand, places it to the inside of my right thigh, and presses it toward him as he says, "Use your right elbow to push your knee back. Great. Now sink deeper and deeper; feel the opening in your hips." He comes in even closer to me and whispers in my ear, "Feel that, Cass?" I take a long inhalation, and as I exhale he whispers again, "Do you feel that?"

Speaking to the whole class now, he abruptly moves away from me and says authoritatively, "Change—other side."

Bastard! He knew exactly what he was doing, and the hell of it is—it worked. Nothing's changed. Mark was wrong. I was wrong. I'm not stronger, better, different—not when it comes to Daniel! That charge, that electricity, that want is still there, maybe even stronger than before.

Like a maestro conducting the philharmonic, he skillfully guides us through the rest of class. He's just given an amazing class, and he knows it, so confident, even a bit arrogant. I think back to my first class with him. That exhilaration, that excitement, is back, so very, very back.

After class I quickly change and practically sprint out of the studio. I whisk by Daniel and thank him for class without looking at him. I get in my car and sit for a while. This can't be happening again. Living in my little cocoon for so long and being what Mark called a recluse insulated me from the world and from the feelings of pain and loss, but it also insulated me from other feelings like the ones I just experienced with Daniel. I guess for a long time, without realizing it, I was putting on a charade, for Steve, for my kids, and for my family. Pretending everything was fine on the outside, but on the inside I was dying a slow death, just like my father. I was going through the motions of life. Getting through the day was a huge accomplishment. Mark couldn't have been more right. I'm existing, not living. My cell phone rings. It's Mark.

"Hey, Mark, thought you were on a date?"

"Yeah, I did too. Felt more like an AA meeting. Talk about baggage. That guy comes with his own conveyer belt system. I had to get out of there. Another hour with him and you'd have been attending one more memorial service!"

I laugh. "Mark, can I come by?"

"Really, you have to ask? Of course!" he says.

By the time I get to Mark's, I'm all worked up again. He pours us some wine. I'm pacing in his living room back and forth. Mark finally says, "Cass, could you stop pacing? You're making me dizzy. What's wrong with you? He was cold again, wasn't he? What is it with that guy? Just don't go to his classes, avoid him completely, and if you do see him be polite but distant. You don't need this." I don't answer. "Cass, are you listening to me? Just stop going when he teaches, no big deal. He'll eventually mellow and realize how immature he's being."

I walk up and push both my hands into Mark's chest; his wine almost spills. "You were right the other day. This is your fault. All that stronger, better, different crap!" I shout. "You can do this, Cass, you and me together!" I say, mimicking him. "Right, Mark? Right?"

"Yeah," he says confused, "right."

"Wrong. No, wrong!" I explode. "I'm weak and pathetic, just like we talked about before. Gullible, pliable, mush in his hands."

Mark takes me by the hand and sits me down on the couch. "OK, stop. Tell me what happened from the beginning, like from the second you walked in the door."

I recount every detail, leaving nothing out. Then I tell him about Triangle pose, the stretch, the touch, the whisper. Mark brings both his hands toward his face and covers his mouth.

"Oh shit," he says. "Now I'm getting turned on."

"Be serious, Mark!" I demand.

"Ah, I am," he says, smiling.

I get up from the couch and start pacing. "Why is this happening again? I was perfectly content—dodging, avoiding— and now this! Things have been going so much better since I've been back to yoga. My relationship with Steve is better, and the sex has been good. Granted he's still not the greatest communicator, but neither am I. This past year he's been so strong for me, even when I was being horrible and shutting him out. Patiently he waited, listened, and did everything he could to get me through that horrific time, and how do I repay him? By nearly climaxing in Triangle, that's how!" I look over at Mark, and he's obviously resisting the urge to laugh. I pick up a pillow from the couch and throw it at him. "Mark, stop. This isn't funny!"

He laughs and says, "Triangle pose, who knew?" He's laughing openly now. I lighten up and smile, shaking my head at him.

Eighteen

It's been a couple of months since Daniel so famously proved to me how nothing between us had died. It may have been denied or dormant, but the intensity of our attraction toward each other is alive and strong. I don't try to avoid his classes anymore. If a class works for my schedule and he happens to be teaching it, I go. The iciness comes and goes but for the most part is gone.

We're back to where we were before the calls, the texts, the tea, and trips to the mountains and beach. We exchange flirtatious glances, tease each other, and practice next to each other when we can. When he's teaching he'll give me a gentle touch here and there disguised as an adjustment, and then he'll flash me that knowing grin. It's playful, innocent, and fun. He hasn't brought up getting together again and never calls or texts, so that's been somewhat of a relief. I mean, what's there to say, really? It's not like this thing between us can go anywhere. Some things are just better left alone.

Of course, that doesn't take away from the fact that I think about him all the time, especially that moment we shared on the beach. It always brings a smile to my face. Strange, as confusing as this is sometimes, I'm happier, more alive, since meeting

Daniel, especially these past four months since I've been back to yoga. Life doesn't feel like such a grind filled with mundane, mindless details. Whether I see him or not, I look forward to my days with excitement and anticipation.

My sex life with Steve has reached new heights. Granted I go back and forth between being present, enjoying the moment with Steve, and letting my mind be swept away with thoughts of Daniel. I'm much more vocal with Steve about what I want in the bedroom. "Softer kisses, Steve. Kiss my neck. Slow down. Touch me here like this," I say. He's more than happy to oblige and is loving what he's receiving. I feel liberated, free, and confident. I'm finding a voice I never knew I had.

Since my dad passed, I've distanced myself from my mom and Allison while simultaneously building this incredible relationship with William. I'm having so much fun discovering him; he's truly brilliant. Like Mark, he helps me see myself in a way that's authentic and unfiltered. We talk or text almost every day. He makes me think; he makes me laugh. The bond between us that started when Andy was diagnosed has grown stronger and stronger. After losing both Andy and my dad, I've realized life is too short and too long for relationships that create a burden or heaviness in my heart. I don't have room for emotional manipulations or doing things out of guilt or shame. At some point you either become buried alive by all that shit—so you may as well be dead—or you turn that shit into compost and grow yourself a beautiful garden.

If someone had told me a year ago that I'd be where I am today, I never could've believed it was possible. I'd have been pleased to just get back to where I was pre-Andy-cancer phase, but I'm truly, for the first time in my life, happier, more confident, more alive, than I've ever been. Gone are the days of coaxing myself to yoga and all the angst and insecurity that went with it. My practice has improved exponentially, and on the mat I'm freer and not afraid to fall out of a posture or, heaven forbid, lose my composure. I'm becoming fearless. I've realized I can't spend my whole life living "as if." As if some people or some things are different. That "as if" was suffocating me and stunting any chance I had of living a genuine life.

In families we do that "as if" thing quite a bit. It starts in childhood, and then we spend our whole adult lives trying to figure out who we are and who we were meant to be before the "as ifs" got a hold of us. If we're lucky enough, we figure it out, but many of us stay stuck, usually in anger and playing the blame game. I believe the only way to get unstuck is by going in, deep within, and tapping into the part of ourselves that we never talk about, the part that's hidden, the part we'd rather forget about. If we do that, we can slowly begin to peel back the layers of perceived shame and guilt. Then we have the opportunity to confront the discomfort head on and face the fears holding us back. We take back the lives that were meant to be ours and start seeing ourselves as we really are and as the person we've always been. We reach a point where we no longer buy into the trappings of what someone or some people said we were or are.

In my experience when you go through great loss, either something inside of you dies and you become bitter or something blossoms and an awakening occurs. Some people, unfortunately, get lodged in grief. I was there for a while, feeling paralyzed and consumed with sadness. I felt like a deep-sea diver whose leg somehow got trapped between rocks or coral. I could look up and see some light shining on the water above but couldn't seem to get free. Fortunately, instead of giving up and succumbing to what seemed like an inevitable fate, I kept going to yoga and doing the things I knew would make me feel better. A very wise yogi told me once, "Yoga is like mathematics: it can't fail. Trust the yoga; it won't fail you." Finally, I was free and floated weightlessly to the top.

Now I'm experiencing a blossoming, an awakening, a new beginning, not because Andy or my dad would have wanted it that way, not for Steve or for my kids. It's not even conscious; it's on a level much deeper than that. It's a joy, an inner peace, and a knowing that, no matter what, all is as it's meant to be in this very moment. All that's happened has happened exactly as it was meant to happen. How can I say that? The answer is simple: because that's the way it happened. Once I accepted that, I wasn't stuck anymore. That acceptance, that surrender, is what allowed me to move forward with my life. Andy and my father are free; their souls have moved on. I believe that with everything I am. I've decided I don't want to wait for death to be free; I want it in the here and now.

⌒

*E*arly Sunday morning I head to one of my favorite places: the farmers' market. Steve took Joey and Lance to Disneyland for the day. He's meeting his brother, Matt, and his kids there. I have the whole day and even most of the evening to myself. I walk around the farmers' market, taking in all the scents of different herbs and fresh vegetables and fruits. I feel so content and at peace. There are very few things in this world that are perfect. Fruits, vegetables, herbs, and spices—now that's perfection, proof of life, proof of something much bigger than us. You don't have to look further than a farmers' market on a Sunday morning to see the beauty and miracle of life.

I walk over to the table with herbs and pick up some fresh oregano and basil. They're so fresh and fragrant. From behind me I hear someone say, "Hi, Cass." My heart skips a beat. I feel a flutter in my stomach; I know immediately it's Daniel. As I turn to say hello, the happiness I feel to see and hear him is obvious.

"Daniel, hi," I say, trying to catch my breath. I start to walk away from the herb table and ask, "How are you?"

Without answering my question, he says, "Cass, I feel like I owe you an apology. I mean, I know things are kind of better now, but before I was so cold—still am sometimes. It was just hard after not—"

I interrupt him and say understandingly, "First, thank you for that, but Daniel, in our situation—and I don't want this to sound harsh or unfeeling—we really don't owe each other explanations."

He changes the subject. "Are Steve and the kids here with you?"

"No," I respond, "this isn't really their thing. How about Cheryl? Is she here?"

"No, not really her thing either." Some of the things Daniel and I have discovered we share are a passion for cooking, rain forests, hiking, music, farmers' markets, and, of course, yoga.

We walk for a while, trying to make small talk; the silent moments between us are uncomfortable. "Cass, can we talk, I mean just talk, nothing else? I really would like to clear the tension," he says clumsily, not his usual, confident self.

Which tension? I think, smiling. *The sexual tension? I don't think it's conversation that will clear that up.* I know what he means though, and I respond sincerely, "Yes, we can talk." So, here I am, standing in the middle of this bustling farmers' market, people whizzing by us, waiting for him to say something. "Dan," I finally say, "well, talk."

"No, no, Cass. Not here. Not like this," he asserts. Has he completely lost touch with reality? He can't mean alone.

"Daniel, no," I say firmly. "Not alone. No. No. Not alone." Has he forgotten what happens when we're alone, especially the last time we were alone?

"Cass, nothing will happen, I promise. I just want to talk," he says emphatically.

Staring at him, I see how incredibly sincere he is. He truly wants some kind of—and I hate the term—closure. Things have been left open-ended like a *dot, dot, dot*. He wants to fill in some blanks and put a period at the end of our sentence. I guess I kind of like having things open ended, but it's clearly making Daniel crazy. I love the anticipation of not knowing, the exhilaration and thrill that comes with this unfulfilled sexual tension between us. I don't want it to end, at least not yet. Milan Kundera, the one who wrote *The Unbearable Lightness of Being*, said, "Flirting is like the promise of sexual intercourse without a guarantee." That's what's made these past months so exciting. It's like really great foreplay without the guilt. In that moment I realize how selfish I'm being. He needs this to be put to rest, and if I owe him anything, I owe him that.

"OK, Daniel, where would you like to go?"

He exhales, relieved, and says sincerely, "Thanks, Cass. Let's just drive up the coast and see where we land." He smiles, with glimmers of hope in his eyes.

"Let's take my car, but you drive," I say, tossing him my keys.

"Deal!" he agrees.

We walk to my car and get in. He looks good in my driver's seat. "Daniel," I say adamantly, "just so we're clear: nothing can happen." He tries to say something, but I continue, "And after this, I don't want to be bashed upside the head again with another iceberg."

"Cass, we're past that. Let's just have a relaxing drive and"— referring to our last time together—"enjoy this moment in time."

꒰ ꒱

As we make our way farther and farther up the coast, I know we're going to the same place as before. It makes sense. The beach is far enough away that the odds of someone seeing us are small. Especially with Daniel's two studios and countless students, we can't take any chances. This particular stretch of beach is very, very secluded. Last time we were there, I don't remember seeing anyone.

I start to feel myself getting anxious and having second thoughts about this. Daniel reaches his hand out to turn off the radio, and I reactively jerk away from him. "What's wrong, Cass?" he asks, puzzled, as he parks the car.

Oh no, we're here, I think. My heart is pounding out of my chest. "Daniel, this isn't a good idea. Please, let's go back. We can talk on the drive." I can barely get the words out fast enough, as if I'm in a race against time.

"Relax," he says soothingly. "Breathe, Cass. Breathe."

I angrily reply, "Dammit, Daniel, this isn't yoga class. This is our lives. I mean, out here with you again, like this, it's wrong, just wrong!"

He gets out of the car and comes to the passenger-side door. *What's he doing?* I think. *Hasn't he heard a word I just said?*

He calmly opens my door, reaches for my hand, and slowly pulls me toward him out of the car and says reassuringly, "Yes, Cass, that's why we're here. Let's talk about the wrong and anything else we feel like. Just talk."

I'm realizing just how little I trust myself alone with him and this pull of desire I feel for him. *Is he counting on that,* I wonder, *or does he sincerely just want that ridiculous closure thing everyone always talks about?* I step out of the car and slip my hand out of his. We walk down the steep embankment toward the shoreline. I'm wishing it was overcast and gloomy with a chance of rain, but no, another glorious day—not too hot, not too cool—with a gentle ocean breeze.

We stop at the shore, and facing me, he takes his hair out of his ponytail, knowing how much I love it when he wears it down. What's he doing? I still can't catch my breath. The attraction I feel toward him is overpowering. We shouldn't be here. "Now you," he says with a boyish grin.

"Now me what?" I question, confused.

"Take your hair down," he says.

"Take my hair down?" I ask, grinning, tilting my head to one side.

"Yeah, take your hair down," he says again playfully. I take my hair down and shake it out. "There," he states, "that's better. Come on. Let's walk for a while." I hesitate. "Don't worry, Cass. Just walk, nothing else," he teases. I feel my defenses come down a bit. "So, how have you been?" he asks. "I mean with the deaths of your brother and father. You must've gone through hell."

I reply, "You know, Dan, grief is weird. It's a very solitary experience…not lonely, just solitary. There really aren't any words that do it justice. Even though Steve, Mark, and William were there for me—"

He interrupts, "I wanted to be there for you, Cass. I really did. I felt shut out."

I try to explain. "I had to shut you out, Dan. There was no letting you in at that point."

"Why?" he asks. "I mean, even just as a friend?"

"A friend?"

"Yeah, as a friend."

I can't believe he's saying that. "You and I have never been just friends, not ever," I say directly. "How do we go from that day on the beach and everything that led up to that day to just friends?" Then I add sarcastically, "'Steve, this is Daniel, just a friend.' Come on, really?"

He comes back with, "Mark was there for you."

"Of course Mark was there for me. We started as friends and will always be just friends."

He bitterly remarks, "That's not what I hear." The rumors did get back to him.

"Yeah, what did you hear?" I ask, knowing. He doesn't answer. "What, Daniel? What did you hear, that we're having an affair?"

Angrily he responds, "Yeah, Cassandra, that's what I heard, from quite a few people in fact. All the hugging, kissing, whispering in each other's ears, laughing, and carrying on—I heard it all! Then to make things worse"—his voice is really rising now—"you bring him into my studio, purposely avoiding me, and throw it in my face!" I'm taken aback by his directness and anger. I'm even more taken aback that he thinks I could do that. I can't respond. "Say something!" he commands.

"What do you want me to say to that, Dan? Really, what do I say to that?" Now I'm angry. "Mark's the least of what should be our concern. How about Steve? How about Cheryl? How about the four children between us? What of that? Your biggest concern is Mark? Do you even hear yourself?"

He won't let up. "Are you sleeping with him, Cass?" he asks, hands on his hips and a look on his face I've never seen before. I'm quiet. "I have to know," he continues. "Are you? Is that why it was so easy for you to walk away from me?" *He can't be serious. He must be joking.* Again he asks slowly but angrily, enunciating and pausing between each word, "Are…you…sleeping…with… him?"

"Mark and I—" I begin to explain, but I can't even get any more words out.

He points his finger at me, arm straight out, his other hand still on his hip, and shouts, "Don't say that!" Even louder he says again, "Don't say that!"

I yell back, "Don't say what?" I'm not only very upset at this point but also really confused. "Don't say, 'Mark and I,'" he yells. "What's this 'Mark and I' shit?"

Throwing my hands up into the air, I blurt out, "He's gay, for Christ's sake!"

There's a stunned silence now. Daniel looks completely perplexed. "Gay?" he asks, surprised.

"Yes, gay," I reply.

"I didn't know," he responds, sounding flustered.

"Obviously!" I exclaim.

"He doesn't seem, well—"

I cut him off. "Don't even go there, Dan. Don't."

"Gay? Wow," he says under his breath.

"Can we drop it now?" I ask him.

"Yeah, yeah, of course," he says, still taking it all in.

We continue walking a few more minutes without talking. Daniel then says, "I can't tell you how crazy that was making me. I could barely eat. I couldn't sleep. I care about you, Cassandra. I care a lot, and the thought of another man—I mean, not Steve… well, him too, but—"

I help him out. "Dan, it's OK. I know. I wouldn't like it either if I thought you were with someone other than Cheryl—well, her too, but you know." We both know and smile at each other.

"You're something, Cassandra. I couldn't have ever imagined feeling this way about someone." His vulnerability and openness disarm me even more.

"I feel the same way, Daniel, more than I care to admit."

He steps in closer to me, reaches out his hand, brushes the windswept hair from my face. "God, you're beautiful, Cass." Then he looks into my eyes with his palm gently touching my cheek. I press my cheek into his palm, close my eyes, and take a deep breath. I think about how much I love and miss his tenderness and touch.

I force myself to pull away and start to walk away from him, down the beach again. He follows closely by my side. Our hands lightly touch every once in while, until Daniel finally takes a hold of my index finger with his. He pauses and looks at me as if he's asking, "Is this OK?" I smile, and so does he. We continue walking, only now the silence is comfortable and welcome.

Daniel finally breaks the silence, asking, "What are we going to do about this?"

I quickly respond, "Nothing. There's nothing we can do."

"Is that what you really believe?" he asks.

"It's what I know," I say with resolve.

"What about all this between us? Do we just toss it aside and pretend it's not there?"

"That's what we do, Daniel. Think about it—combined we have over thirty-four years of marriage, and on top of that four kids, mine still at home. Do we toss *that* aside and pretend *that's* not there? I just can't see that part of us spontaneously combust. It's not fair to Steve, Cheryl, or our kids." He knows I'm right. He sighs and nods his head.

We walk hand and hand for what is, more than likely, our last time alone together. Daniel suddenly pulls me, almost forcibly, toward him, puts his arms around my waist, and pulls me close to him. My hands are on his shoulders, and I'm pushing him away slightly. He resists and pulls me in even closer, his arms tight around my waist. Here we are again, bodies pressed against each other, forehead to forehead, history repeating itself, only this time it's more intense, less tender.

Still holding me tight with one arm, he takes his other hand, lifts my chin, and without hesitation or caution, begins kissing me. I give in for a few moments but quickly come to my senses. I push him away and step back. "No!" I cry out. "You promised, Daniel. You promised nothing would happen!" I'm almost sobbing.

"Yes, I did promise nothing would happen," he replies non-apologetically. "But this, Cass—this between us—this isn't nothing. This is something, something very real, very powerful, very strong, very beautiful. Is it wrong? No, it isn't wrong. The circumstances may make it wrong, but what we feel—that's not wrong. Hell, it isn't even right; it just is."

I brush my hands through my hair and look up toward the sky, feeling completely torn apart. "No, Daniel, no!" I rapidly start walking back toward the car.

"Cass!" he yells. "Don't walk away from me again!" I ignore him. "Cassandra!" he shouts again.

I don't look back, and I walk even faster. Tears fill my eyes. I begin to slow down. Tears are now pouring down my face. I stop, put my hands on my knees, and try to pull myself together. I turn to see where he is. He's still standing where I left him, hands on his hips, looking down. *Keep going, Cass. Don't go back. Keep going. Keep going,* I try frantically to convince myself. *Dammit, don't do it, Cass!*

But it doesn't work. I look back. I start walking toward him, slowly at first. He looks up. I want desperately to be in his arms again. I start almost jogging, and he begins walking fast toward me. We meet and embrace, holding each other so tightly, neither one of us wanting to let go. We pause, look at each other, and simultaneously begin to kiss feverishly, passionately, all the pent-up desire completely unleashed. I'm holding his face; he's holding mine. We stop for a moment. I trace my fingers along his face and lips. He lovingly kisses my tears away. Again, we begin kissing, only now softly, gently, and with a tenderness that, this time, transcends all that's careless, all that's wrong, and all that's forbidden between us.

We both sense someone approaching us, and we break away. It's an older couple, maybe in their seventies. We notice them smiling at us. We smile back, embarrassed by our public display of affection. "Cass," Daniel says.

"Dan, please, let's not talk about what this is, where it's going, and what we're going to do about it—"

He breaks in, smiling. "Cassandra, I just want to know what time you have to be back."

"Oh," I say, feeling silly. "Steve is in Anaheim with the kids and won't be back till later tonight, but I told Mark I'd stop by after the farmers' market."

"Is there any way you can cancel that?" he asks.

"Dan, aren't you teaching class later this afternoon?"

"Yeah, but I'm sure I can find someone to cover."

"OK," I say, shrugging my shoulders. We both go our separate ways and pull out our cell phones, trying to find reception. I call Mark and get his voice mail. I leave him a message that I won't be able to make it and will touch base later.

Dan calls out, "Any luck, Cass?"

"Yeah," I say, "come try over here." He walks over to where I'm standing. I walk away, giving him privacy, assuming he needs to call Cheryl as well.

I text Steve and tell him I'm at the beach now and hope they're having a good time. He texts back a picture of all of them that says, "Wish you were here. We love you!"

"Love you too," I text back. Pangs of guilt try to make their way to the surface. I callously push them aside. I want this day—maybe even *need* this day—just this day, without fear, without guilt, without expectations. There'll be plenty of time for all of that later. It's strange how once you cross certain boundaries, it makes it easier to cross other, more dangerous ones. It's probably better to never go there.

I sit on the beach, waiting for Daniel. We humans have become masters at the art of justifications to ease our guilty souls. Last time we were here, I rationalized, "Well, it's not like we really, really kissed. We embraced, he gave me some sweet kisses, and then our lips briefly touched a few times." Boundaries crossed, definitely, but was it fatal? No, not really. Now this. I'm still working on a really good justification for this one. The longer Daniel takes, the more time I have to create some really good fiction to convince myself it's all still OK. It sounds something like this, "Well, we never took our clothes off. We really just kissed—albeit passionately—but most of all, we didn't have any real sexual contact beyond that." That's lame fiction, Bill Clinton–kinda stuff, but it'll have to do for now. If Steve did any of that, any part of it, I'd be devastated.

Daniel walks over toward me and says, "Done, class covered." I want to ask him what he told Cheryl, but we rarely bring up Steve and Cheryl—ironically, out of respect for them. That's sacred territory. We talk in vague generalities, but it's all benign stuff.

"Are you hungry?" he asks.

"Starving!" I exclaim.

"I know this great place not far from here, plenty for us to choose from," he says, excited, as he pulls me up by hands. Daniel's vegetarian and I'm vegan, so it's nice to go somewhere that can accommodate us.

When we pull up to the restaurant—more like a stand—it's crowded. I tell Daniel to order for both of us, and I'll wait in the car. He agrees that would be best. The reality of who we are and what we are to each other and others isn't lost on us. We know it, we get it, and we don't try to pretend otherwise. "What would you like, Cass?" he asks.

"I don't know. Surprise me," I say, smiling. I'm almost sure he's going to come back with either a falafel or hummus sandwich, burger, or burrito. That's most places' idea of accommodating vegans. I've had so much of it when we vacation that I quite literally can't stomach the stuff anymore. I mentioned that once to Daniel, so I'm curious to see what he gets.

He goes up to the stand and, considering how busy they appear to be, comes back fairly quickly. He gets in the car, puts the bag of food in the backseat, and pulls away. I ask him what he got. "It's a surprise," he says, grinning. Whatever it is, it smells delicious.

We go back to the beach and park in the same place as before. "Let's eat in the car," Daniel says. "Sand and food don't go well together."

I agree. I open the bag and ask, "Which one is mine?"

"They're both the same. Take your pick."

"Going vegan today, Dan?"

"Anything for you, Cass," he replies sweetly. I hand him one and take the other out of the bag. There are also two half-pint containers in there; he tells me it's herbed potato salad. There are also two waters, room temperature. He has this thing about cold water, says it messes with the digestive system, an Ayurvedic thing. He still sometimes calls me out in class for having ice in my coconut water. I open the foil packaging of what looks like a burrito and take a bite. *Yum,* I think, *and not falafel or hummus.* I take another bite to get a better look of what's inside: grilled vegetables, tofu, lots of shitake and button mushrooms, and brown rice in a ginger sauce. I've just died and gone to culinary heaven. It's perfectly spiced with a hint of heat that hits you right at the end. The mushrooms are perfection. Mushrooms, to me, should be their own food group on the food pyramid. Mushrooms, then everything else.

"Well?" he asks. He hasn't even taken a bite; he's just watching me, waiting for a response.

"This is on their menu?" I ask him.

"No, I ordered off menu, what I think are some of your favorites," he replies.

I give him a big smile, lean in, and give him a kiss on the cheek. "You did good, Dan. This is truly delicious!"

"I did good? That's good," he says proudly, more to himself than to me. We finish most of our burritos and part of our salads.

"Maybe we should head back?" I say halfheartedly.

"Not a chance. Come on, let's go back down to the beach." He gets out of the car, and just like before, opens my door, takes my hand, and pulls me out. He holds me close, kisses my forehead, and says softly, "I never want to let you go."

"I know," I say with a sigh. I'm feeling melancholy, knowing this day will end, my life of details will resume, and Daniel and I will be once upon a time with no happily ever after, at least not with each other.

We make our way down to the beach, the melancholy replaced with joy and freedom. Everything else can wait, but not this moment, not this day, not this time with Dan. I'm filled to the brim with everything that's him: his boyish charm, his tenderness, his laughter, his passion.

He heads down to the shoreline and crouches to look at something. I approach him to see what he's looking at. It's a sand dollar in perfect condition. He asks me if I know the legend of the sand dollar. I shake my head. He explains, "Do you see these five slits on the edge? Well, these are supposed to represent the five wounds on the body of Jesus. Look here, Cass"—he points to the center of the sand dollar—"this is a five-pointed star. This is said to represent the Star of Bethlehem, and here on the back— see here?—this looks like a poinsettia, the flower of Christmas." He breaks open the shell and continues. "These five pieces of calcium that look like little birds, the story goes, these are doves. And when the sand dollar is broken open, they're released to spread joy, peace, and goodwill throughout the world."

"That's a really beautiful story, Dan. I'll never look at a sand dollar in quite the same way again," I say, trying not to laugh.

"You're mocking me, aren't you?" he asks playfully. "I'm being mocked."

"It's kind of like that story you tell us in class about the yogi who stood in Tree Pose for a thousand years and had all these vines and weeds growing up through him and around him," I say tauntingly.

"Hey, that's a true story!" he says, laughing.

"Oh yeah, that's a true story! Did this guy like not know anybody? Don't you think someone would have said, 'You know I haven't seen Pranav in oh about'"—I pretend to look at a watch on my wrist—"'twenty years or so. Anyone know where he is?' 'Oh, probably in Tree Pose in a field somewhere with vines and weeds growing all around him.' 'Oh that Pranav, he's such a character!'" I'm having fun teasing him. "And by the way, Dan—you've never been clear in class—is this guy alive or dead when they find him? How do they know it's been a thousand years? Does he have rings around him like trees get? After all, he was in Tree Pose."

Dan is very amused and exclaims, "It's symbolic and in the ancient texts!"

"Symbolic?" I say, chuckling. "Symbolic of what? Having no life so he decides to stand on one leg for eternity?"

He laughs and lunges toward me. I try to get away, but he catches me. We fall back, and he's on top of me now. "You're just like that sand dollar, Cassandra, every bit like it. How many people do you ever let break you open to see the joy, beauty, vulnerability, and peace that's inside of you?" he says, gently touching my face.

"You've broken me open, Dan," I reply softly. He starts kissing me, first my lips, then my neck. He takes my hands and places them over my head, our fingers interlocked. His kisses move further down to my chest. He lets go of one hand and touches my breast, gently caressing it as he kisses my neck again. I feel him rubbing against me. I release my other hand. With both hands free now, I lift the back of his T-shirt and run my hands all along his bare back.

The soft moans he's making, the way he's slowly rubbing on me and kissing me, have me insane with desire. I want to feel our bodies naked, nothing between us. "I want you, Cass," he says, breathing heavily. "I have to have you, if only just once."

I take his shirt off and move him onto his back. I start kissing him all over, starting with his cheeks, then moving to his eyes, then lips. I move down to his neck and chest. He feels and smells so good. I start to kiss all around his stomach, taking my time, lightly teasing him with my tongue. I straddle him, my knees on either side of his hips. I take his hands and hold them tightly above his head. I stare into his eyes for a few moments, then slowly make my way back to his lips, my hair flowing freely and all around him. We kiss again. I'm now rubbing against him, and all I can think of is how much I want him inside me, making love to me. Of course that isn't possible.

I move off of him and lie next to him, holding his hand. Both of us are looking up at the sky. So this is what reckless abandon feels like. I look over at Dan and notice a tear dropping from the corner of his eye. "Dan," I say, almost whispering, as I sit up on my elbows, "are you OK?"

He quickly rubs his eyes and says, "Yeah, yeah, Cass, I'm fine. Really, I'm fine." I put my head on his shoulder. He puts his arm around me and holds me close. We don't speak. Like with grief, there are no words that will do justice for this moment and how we're feeling.

⌒

As the sun begins to set, we decide to head back. Once we get in the car, I check my phone and see a text from Steve. Thankfully it's only from a few minutes ago: "Kids want to sleep at Matt and Amy's. You OK with that? How was your day?"

I reply, "What about school? Had a good day."

He texts back, "Teacher conferences, no school."

"That's right, forgot. Fine then. See you guys tomorrow. Give the kids a hug and kiss for me. Love you."

He responds, "Love you, too, baby. I'll call later."

I'm relieved to have tonight alone to somehow process all that's happening. I'm not sure how I'm going to face Steve or even the kids for that matter.

Dan is really quiet, hand on my thigh as he drives. Occasionally he looks over at me, shakes his head from side to side, half smiling, and sighs. "Cassandra," he finally says, "I don't know about you, but I don't know how to let this go. Even when it was let go, I couldn't let go. Now this, after experiencing you in this way, kissing you, touching you, feeling you, being so close to you, it makes me want you, need you—" He pauses.

No, Dan! I scream inside my head. *Don't say it, Dan. Don't you dare say it. Please, God, don't let him say it!*

He continues, "Care about you more." I inhale deeply and exhale, relieved. Let's not cross the love barrier. Want, need, care I can handle; love takes it to a whole new threshold. Besides, this can never happen again. I promise myself, never again!

*   *   *

We pull up to his car, and he asks me to wait for a minute. He gets out and walks to his car, and I move over to the driver's seat. He comes back with something in his hand. He gets in the passenger's seat and says, "I've had this for a long time and have been wanting to give it to you. It's just never been the right time." He hands me a long, rectangular blue velvet box. I open it, and inside there's a necklace with a matching bracelet. I pick up the necklace. It has these lovely moss green and salmon-colored gemstones; in the center is what looks like an ancient coin.

He explains, "The stones are unakite; it means growing together. It's a combination of green epidote and red jasper. The epidote is believed to increase personal power, clear away repressed emotions, and help any healing process. The red jasper is for protection and grounding; it helps during times of conflict and is said to remove blockages from the heart chakra. When the two are combined, they're bound together tightly. So, the meaning is, 'What comes together, belongs together.'" He's speaking calmly but with so much passion.

He continues, "This in the center is an ancient Chinese coin. It's the coin of the five blessings: longevity, health, wealth, love, and a natural death in old age." I'm hanging on to every word he says. "That's my wish for you, Cassandra, the five blessings. No matter what happens, that's my wish for you always."

I stare at the necklace, shaking my head from side to side. I feel a lump in my throat and fight back tears. *No more crying, Cass. Enough with the crying.* This is so not like me. I look up at him, managing for now to keep the tears at bay and ask, "Did you order this off menu as well?"

"Yes," he responds. "I had it made for you." I can't remember the last time I received a gift that was so well thought out.

I move toward him and kiss him sweetly and tenderly on the lips. As it starts to get more passionate, I slowly pull away and say, "Thank you, Daniel. Thank you for thinking of me the way you do."

He gives me one last kiss and whispers in my ear, "Good night, Cass, and thank you for giving me this moment in time." With that, he gets out of the car.

I start to drive away, and I can't hold back the tears any longer. I cry all the way home, not just for Daniel, but for Steve, Joey, Lance, Cheryl, Brandon, and Leah. I'm sure the magnitude of what I did will hit me even harder later, but for now this is all I can handle.

Nineteen

I get home. My head hurts from all the crying, and my heart aches. I pour myself a glass of wine, go upstairs, and draw myself a warm bath. I sit on the edge of the tub, waiting for it to fill. I can still smell Daniel. I'm trying to absorb what I just did. This won't end well; these things never do. Daniel and I—what we did today has the potential for so much collateral damage. What kind of mother am I to not protect my children from something like this? It's a mother's job to protect her children. Sure, we can't protect them from everything, but we certainly can protect them from the preventable. This falls into the category of preventable disasters. The craziest part— the craziest part of all—is even with that knowledge, I miss Daniel already. I wish he were here with me right now, sipping wine and sharing a bath with me.

My phone rings. I think it's Steve and don't want to answer. I look down at it. It isn't Steve; it's Daniel. I'm happy it's him. "Hi, Daniel."

"Hey, Cass. I just wanted to make sure you got home OK," he says, speaking very quietly.

"How are you, Dan? Really, how are you?" I ask.

"Missing you. How about you, Cass?"

"Missing you, too, Dan."

"Are Steve and the kids back?"

I don't want to tell him they're staying overnight in Anaheim. If he knew, I'd be inviting him over or asking him to meet me somewhere. Then what we'd end up doing would make what we did at the beach seem tame in comparison.

"No, not yet. Is Cheryl there?" I ask.

"Yeah, she's outside with a friend of hers on the patio. Wish I was there with you, anywhere with you." I start thinking if he could get away, this would be a great opportunity for us to be together, the way we couldn't be together this afternoon. Should I tell him I have this night free? Could he get away? I really shouldn't even put him in that position. But I want to be with him, I want to kiss him again, feel him again, and so much more.

"Daniel?"

"Yes, Cass."

"Umm, I was wondering if—" I pause.

"What is it, Cass?"

Another call comes through. It's Mark. I tell Daniel I'll call him back, that I have to take this call. He says to make sure I call back; he wants to know what I was going to ask him. I tell him I will and then switch over to take Mark's call.

"Mark, you couldn't have called at a more perfect time. I almost made the biggest mistake of my life! Well, I already made a huge one, but this—this would have been monumental," I say, panicked.

"Cass, you were with him again, weren't you?" he says disapprovingly.

"Yes, Mark, I was," I respond like a child who's just been caught doing something she shouldn't.

"Are Steve and the kids home yet from Disneyland?" he asks.

"No, they're spending the night at Matt and Amy's. Daniel and I ran into each other at the farmers' market and ended up spending the whole day together, and things got, well, pretty heated. He doesn't know they aren't coming home tonight, but when you called I was about to tell him to see if he wanted to get together—not here necessarily, because that would just be rude, but somewhere," I say anxiously. "Mark, I told Daniel I'd call him back so let me call you back."

"That won't be necessary, Cass. Don't call me back." *What? Why would Mark say that? Is he that disappointed with me?*

"Why, Mark?" I ask timidly.

"Go ahead, call Daniel back. Finish your conversation with him. I'm on my way over to spend the night."

I sigh in relief. "Yeah, Mark, that would be good, really good."

"Yes, it would," he replies sensitively. "See you soon."

"Thanks, Mark."

"Sure, Cass."

I call Daniel back. "Hey, Dan. Sorry about that."

"That's OK. What were you going to ask me?"

"I was just wondering if you're feeling any regrets about to-day," I say, lying, but I am curious if he's feeling that way.

"Regrets, no. Considering our situation, I have mixed feelings, but regret is not one of them. Cass, I'd do it all again and more without hesitation. That's where I'm at with all of this," he says with conviction. "How about you? Do you have regrets?"

"I'm still in the processing stage, but right at the moment, oddly enough, no, no regrets."

"Cass, I have a favor to ask you."

"Sure, Dan. What is it?"

"When you figure out a way to get over this, will you let me know?" he asks sincerely.

I reply, "I'd like to say I have this all figured out, and before today, I kind of thought I did. I thought we could coexist with this attraction, this flirtation. You know, dance around with it but never carry anything out. After today I'm so confused and feeling powerless to do anything, one way or the other.

"Dan, I have to ask you something, and either answer me truthfully or don't answer at all. Either way I'll have my answer. Please, just don't lie to me."

"OK, Cass, of course."

I continue and ask, "Today when we ran into each other at the farmers' market, was it really your intention to just talk, nothing else?" There's a long silence. "Dan?" I ask, not even sure if he's still there.

"I'm thinking, Cass, thinking how to word this."

"OK," I say. "Take your time."

He begins, "First, let me start by saying, everywhere I go, I always hope I'll run in to you. I purposefully go out of my way, going to places where I think you might be. Today it finally happened. I was happy to see you and even happier you were alone. You know I've wanted to talk to you for a long time, but you were reluctant, and considering the idea I had about you and Mark, I didn't push it. When we left the farmers' market I was feeling good that we could finally be alone together to talk, to be alone with you, not in a crowded studio with a bunch of students or the very few moments we have before and after class, really alone to talk."

"Dan, you keep saying 'to talk,' but you aren't answering my question," I say, frustrated.

"Cass, I didn't have a master plan for what happened today, but yes, I wanted what happened today to happen. I think of little else. I wanted it. I've fantasized about it and so much more. So, yes, I wanted more than to just talk, but nothing was going to happen that you didn't want to happen."

Good point, I think. I chose to leave with him. I chose to kiss him. I chose it all, and even though my intention was to just talk, I wanted it as much as he did…and still do.

"Does that answer your question, Cass?"

"Yeah, Dan, it does. Thanks."

"Thanks for what?" he questions.

"Thanks for being honest with me."

"Can I ask you something now, Cass?"

"Sure, go ahead."

"When can I see you again?" he asks softly.

"Well, I plan on going to your six-thirty class on Tuesday," I reply, knowing that's not what he's asking.

"Really, Cass," he states, clearly irritated.

I'm silent. I want to see him alone. If Mark hadn't called, we'd probably be in the full throes of passion this very evening, but I know we shouldn't. I promised myself earlier that this could never happen again. "Dan, I'm not saying no or never. What I want to say is today is a huge leap from where we were. Just give me a little time to process things, OK?"

"Fair enough," Dan responds, satisfied for now.

"Dan, until then, please don't do that hot-cold, push-pull game you play with me," I plead.

"It's not a game, Cass. It's my defenses, a way of protecting myself, kind of like this shield that goes up, but, yeah, I'll work on that."

"Fair enough," I say with a little laugh. "Good night, Dan."

"Sleep well, Cass."

Since Mark's on his way over, I skip the bath and take a quick shower. When he arrives, I can tell he's not very happy with me. "Cass, just tell me you didn't have sex with him," he says very seriously.

"I didn't have sex with him," I respond calmly.

"Did you get naked with him?" he inquires further, still very serious.

"No, I didn't get naked with him," I reply, again calmly. "Mark, why don't I just tell you what happened?"

"No, no, we have to take this at a pace I can handle. I'll ask the questions; you just answer! I have to know how much damage control I have to do here." He's very agitated with me.

"Mark, this isn't some White House scandal we have to spin," I remark.

"Save the sarcasm, Cass. I'm in no mood. So, if you didn't get naked then I'm right to assume there was no oral copulation, right?"

"Oral copulation, Mark? Who even speaks like that unless we're in a court of law or something, which is what this is starting to feel like? No, no oral copulation." Now I find myself getting annoyed.

"Clothes on, right?" he asks.

I reply, "At one point he had his shirt off—well, I took it off of him—but everything else was on."

He gives me an irritated look. "You took his shirt off, Cass?"

"Yes, Mark. Can we knock off the twenty questions? I took his shirt off, we kissed passionately, he touched my breast, and that was basically it," I respond sharply.

"Do you see what's happening? Are you seeing the progression here? Do you realize how dangerously close you are to this whole thing exploding in your face? Who do you think is going to pay, Cass? Who? The kids, that's who! You and Steve—you guys will eventually land on your feet, go your separate ways, but what about your kids? Who's going to navigate that sinking ship for them? Nobody. You know why, Cass? Because sinking ships can't be navigated. Do you get that, or shall I make you a PowerPoint presentation? This thing between you and Daniel is going nowhere but down, and you're going to bring everyone down with you. Is that what you guys really want? Please, spare me the 'we can't help it' bullshit, because that's all it is: bullshit! Enough, Cass. End this thing. End it now. Change studios. Change zip codes. Hell, change country codes if you have to, but end it!" he yells.

"I don't want to end it! And I never said we couldn't help it. Everything we've done has been my choice, our choice! Don't put words in my mouth, Mark!" I yell back.

"Then end it with Steve. You can't have it both ways. Life doesn't work that way!"

We're both shouting. "Then how does it work, Mark? By hanging on so tight to the past that you can't possibly move forward? You're so anchored in what was, what could have been but never was between you and Greg, it's like your legs are cemented in concrete. That's the dead weight you've been carrying around for almost two years now. You think you can come here and school me about life and the way it should be. Please, get over yourself!"

"That was low, Cassandra, really low. How dare you say that to me? I don't want to see you ruin everything that means something to you, and you throw Greg in my face!" He's really pissed now.

"Yeah, Mark, that's what I do, because you don't see how much it hurts me to see you so stuck. You talked before about my existing and not living. What do you think you're doing? You're killing time until Greg wakes up one morning and realizes that you're the best thing that ever happened to him, but at least one of us knows that's never going to happen. And that one of us isn't you! Do the math, Mark! You're sitting back, passively watching your life go by like it's some kind of spectator sport. There are quite a few guys that have come and then gone—some of them really amazing—but you can't even see it because you're so stuck in this time warp called Greg!" I reply vehemently.

"You're trying to divert the attention away from you and onto me; that's what you're doing!" he says angrily.

"No, Mark, what I'm trying to show you is that life isn't a straight line. There are zigzags, curves, detours, and every once in while we get smacked so hard upside the head—like what happened with Andy, my dad, your mom, your dog Chi Chi, and Greg—that we don't know what hit us. We make choices, not always the right ones, but we make them. This thing with Daniel, I don't know exactly what it is. All I know is how it makes me feel. What I feel for him runs deep; it's not just physical, Mark. Normally I'd run as far away as possible from something like this, but this time I choose to run toward it, to feel it, experience it.

"Some people are afraid of heights or jumping out of a plane, so they bungee jump or sky dive, while others just continue living with their fears. Well, I fear intimacy. I fear vulnerability. Daniel makes me feel those things stronger and deeper than I ever have with anyone, even Steve. I'm facing my fear. He's my bungee jump, Mark. He's my skydive." I finish what I have to say calmer.

There's a silence between us for a while before Mark finally asks gently, "Are you in love with him, Cass?"

"I don't know, Mark. I really don't know."

He pulls my head to his shoulder and says soothingly, "Just remember, Cass, life may not be a straight line and is filled with zigzags and unexpected detours, but there are no U-turns. You can't go back and untravel a road that's already been traveled. You have to be careful, or that road could lead you straight to hell. Cass?"

"Yeah, Mark?"

"I was kinda hoping the Hoover Dam was going to break all over your face," he says jokingly.

I laugh and reply, "Sorry, Mark. His kisses are perfection, pure perfection."

"That's what I was afraid of," Marks says with a sigh.

The next morning, I can hardly wait to get to yoga. I leave Mark asleep at the house and head to the studio. Dan isn't teaching, so he should be practicing. I get there first and put my mat down. The blond guy Daniel can't tolerate close to me puts his mat inches from mine and smiles. *Damn*, I think, *I really wanted to practice next to Dan!* The class starts to fill up. *Where is he?* I wonder.

He finally walks in, comes toward me, pauses, and gets this really agitated look on his face. He's thinking about what to do. He can't ask the guy to move; that's not good yoga etiquette. I can't move and find a place where Dan and I could practice together; that would be too obvious. *Just find any place, Dan*, I plead silently, trying to convince him with my eyes. *We can practice together next time.*

"Jeff, you don't mind if I cut in here, do you?" he says. Blond guy has a name? I'm sure I've heard it in class; it's just never stuck. I can't believe what Dan is doing.

"Ah well, Daniel, I kinda—"

Daniel interrupts him. "No, of course you don't mind. Plenty of room. I have to practice here for logistical purposes." I shake my head, smiling. Logistical purposes? Really?

Jeff picks up his mat and says, "Sure, Daniel, no problem."

"Thanks, Jeff. Next class on me, OK, buddy?" Oh, they're buddies now! Dan doesn't say anything to me—class is about to start—he just flashes me that beautiful grin of his.

Practicing next to him is nothing less than amazing. We float from one posture to the next. It feels like we're the only two people in the room. In our final resting pose, Dan gently squeezes my hand and then pulls away. *Be careful, Dan*, I think. *Someone may notice.* I've never seen him so bold, first with Blondie and now the squeeze of my hand. Lying next to him, I relive the events of the day before, when he was on top of me, kissing me, and then I was on top of him. I decide to be bold as well and stretch my hand out until the tips of my fingertips are touching his. I look over at him. He doesn't turn his head or open his eyes, but I see him smiling. I turn away, tune in, and begin my Savasana.

⌒

After class, as I pull into my driveway, I get a text from Daniel: "I think the statute of limitations on 'processing things' is eight to ten hours. Your time limit has clearly expired. So, what's it going to be? Will you meet me at the café tomorrow at nine and we can take a drive up to our spot in the mountains?"

I text back, "Yes."

He responds, "Yes?"

I reply again, "Yes."

He responds, "YES!"

I walk into the house happy. Steve and the kids are home. I excitedly walk over to Lance first and give him a huge hug and then to Joey. I really missed them. Steve comes over and gives me a big hug and kiss. I pull him close and give him an even bigger hug and longer kiss.

"Maybe we should go away more often?" he asks seductively.

Joey says with a look of disdain, "Ah, guys, we're still in the room. Please!"

"Hey, I missed your mom!" Steve exclaims.

"Well, go miss her upstairs or something!" Joey says sarcastically.

"Let's go then." I take Steve upstairs by the hand.

I can hear both kids laughing and saying, "Oh man, gross!"

We've always been open with Joey and Lance about matters of sexuality and tried to teach them that the body is beautiful and nothing to be ashamed of, unlike how I grew up. Sex was never mentioned in our household in a healthy or positive way. There was always a negative connotation attached to it. I don't want my children growing up that way. I want them comfortable in their bodies and aware of their sexuality and the responsibility that comes with that.

When we get upstairs, I get out of my wet yoga clothes and into the shower. My back is to the shower door when I hear it open and Steve coming inside. I can't even remember the last time we took a shower together—probably before Joey was born. I'm happy he's there. I turn to face him. He takes the soap bar from my hand and begins to lather my body, starting with my chest and breasts. Now both our hands are on the bar of soap as I start to lather my hands up and begin rubbing his chest and stomach. I close my eyes and start kissing him, our bodies pressing and rubbing against each other. My mind keeps wandering to Daniel. I try to bring it back, but I keep imagining Daniel and our time on the beach. I fantasize that it is him with me in the shower, caressing, touching, kissing me. I am filled with desire and completely aroused. I tell myself, *Don't speak.* I don't want to accidently say Dan or Daniel. *Just feel, Cass, and go with it. It's only make-believe. It's OK.* Steve is so consumed with what's happening that it heightens my arousal. We both climax almost simultaneously and kiss for a long time afterward. I love Steve and can't seem to make any sense out of my attraction for Daniel.

⟡

fterward, I dry off and sit on the bed with the towel around me. For some reason I can't help but wonder if this is what Cheryl and Daniel do. The thought of that makes me feel a bit sick to my stomach. Even though we never talked about it, I'm sure they make love. Is it as passionate? Is it as intense? Why am I letting myself think about this? How odd is it that I have feelings of jealousy over a man who isn't even my lover? A man who doesn't belong to me in any sense of the word. Yet I feel some ownership, not in a possessive, needy, clingy way. I feel there is a part of Daniel that only I have access to, a part of him that he gives only to me. I feel that because I give that. There is a part of me that only he has access to. He claims that part of me, I claim that part of him, and it will forever be tucked away in our hearts and in our souls, no matter what happens.

Twenty

The next day I take the kids to school and then meet Dan at the café. Like last time, we don't stay, just get a few things and make our way up to the mountains. In the car I immediately bring up Blondie from yoga class. "I can't believe what you did with that guy, Jeff, yesterday."

"Hey, seriously, Cass, I don't even know how you let that guy put his mat so close to yours. I mean, I could understand if it was a full house and everyone is mat to mat, which happens, what, maybe three or four times a year? This clown, there could be ten people in the room, and there he is right on top of you."

"Well, that's better than inferno-breath-orgasm lady who amps it up for you every Saturday," I tease.

"Hey, don't talk about her that way. She can't help it. I have that effect on women!" he says humorously.

"Oh yeah, you have that effect on us. You just walk by, and we all throw ourselves on our mats in heat!" I reply flippantly.

Daniel parks the car. We get out and head toward the trailhead. His arm's around my shoulder, mine around his waist. "Come here, Cass," he says, pulling me to face him. He holds my face with his hands and kisses me. I kiss him back. We get closer, and it gets more intense, our arms around each other's waists now.

I pull away slightly. "Dan," I say softly, looking at him, "we both know this can't lead anywhere."

Lightening things up, Daniel responds, taking me by the hand, "Of course it does, Cass. It leads to a beautiful lake. Come on."

I laugh and follow, wondering how we're going to end this thing. I don't think either one of us has any intention of breaking up our homes, and before we've no choice—like Cheryl or Steve finding out—it needs to end. He says he has no regrets, and so far I haven't felt that way either. Guilt? Remorse? Yes. Regret? No. I guess regret really wouldn't come into play unless this thing explodes in our faces. But if we keep going the way we're going, it will. It's just a matter of time before either Steve or Cheryl figures it out. We always delete our texts and voice mails to each other, but there's bound to be a slipup somewhere along the line. A text will be found, a phone call overheard, maybe someone from the studio sees us somewhere, like here. You just never know. It's better that Daniel and I hurt from the pain of letting go than hurting others because of our own selfishness. But that's my mind talking. When I'm with him, or even when I'm not, I want to feel the emotions. I want the desire and the passion that stirs inside me. I want to make love to him.

Daniel jumps up onto a huge boulder and faces me. "Hey, Cass, come up here. Let's do Standing Bow together."

I climb onto the boulder. I look out, and the view is incredible. The trees are so tall and majestic, and there's a slight fog that runs right through the middle of them. It's a cool, crisp morning; the smell of the pine tress is omnipresent. Standing Bow is one of my favorite postures. It's so elegant and full of grace. It's also known as the Cosmic Dancer, a balancing posture.

Dan instructs, "Face me, Cass. You start on your right leg, and I'll start on my left."

We're mirroring each other. We begin together. We grab the insides of our opposing ankles with our opposite hands while stretching up with our other hands. Then we each begin to kick our free legs back and up behind us as we reach forward with our upstretched hands. As we move into the posture, our palms touch and our eyes lock onto each other. When we reach our balancing stretch, we each create a perfect bow in our backs, with our forward-stretched arms acting as the arrows.

Dan says, "Breathe long and deep, Cass, not normal breathing like in class. Connect to your heart center, to that place inside of you that's expansive and wide open. Now fill that space with all the love and joy that's in you."

We hold the pose for quite a long time, much longer than in class, and then do it again on the opposite side. I'm feeling beautiful, strong, and confident, like I could hold the pose forever, the same feelings I have when I'm with Daniel. I know, though, like in any posture, I'll have to come out, release, and let it go without judgment and without attachment. That day with Daniel's coming. I'll let go; I'll release, without judgment and without attachment.

$\smile$

We walk back to Daniel's car; time always seems to soar by when we're together. Daniel pulls the car out and drives over to a different part of the parking lot where there are no cars. He parks and starts kissing me. He then begins crawling to the backseat. I watch him. He takes my hand and pulls me with him. I smile. This feels like high school, making out in the backseat. He leans into me, and we begin passionately embracing, exploring, kissing, and feeling each other all over. He starts to unbutton my shirt. My black bra is exposed now. He caresses both breasts and kisses right along each one of them. I press on his low back as he rubs against me, pushing my hips up even more to meet his, my head tilting back as he sensually kisses my chest and neck.

"Cass, I need you. I want you."

There's nothing I want more than to be with him completely. "I need you, Dan. I want you. I want to feel you inside me, making love to me." I start to undo his pants, and he helps me. We kiss intensely, both consumed with desire and with each other. His pants are undone but still on. He starts unzipping mine.

Dan stops himself suddenly and gets up, clearly aroused. He pulls his shirt down and brings the front of my shirt together, covering my bra. "Cass, not like this. I don't want our first time to be like this," he says as he runs his hands through his long hair.

"I know, Dan. Neither do I."

Now we've acknowledged there will be a first time. I pull him back toward me and start kissing him again. I can't get enough of him. I feel I can't get close enough. "We don't have to make love. Just kiss me, Dan. Touch me. At least we have this moment right now. Let's not worry about anything else."

He slowly moves toward my lips, starts kissing me, and says, "Open your eyes, Cass. Look at me. Kiss me with your eyes open. I want you to see me. I want you to breathe me. I want to breathe you; I want to see you, deep inside of you."

This takes things to a whole new level of intensity, something I've never felt before. We stare into each other's eyes as we kiss sensuously, lovingly, slowly, and with reverence. The depth of the emotions is tangible, even frightening. My feelings for Dan are so much more than physical; looking into his eyes, I know these feelings are mutual.

He gets up and says, somewhat frustrated, "We have to stop before I can't stop myself. Cass, is there a time you can get away for a night or two?"

A night or two? That escalated quickly, I think to myself. "I don't know, Dan. Maybe we should really think about this," I say, trying to be rational.

"We've been thinking about this for over three years, Cassandra. How long can we keep going on like this? I meant what I said at the beach—I'll be with you, if only just once, but not here in a car, not like this."

I look at him, grinning, with my head slightly to one side, and flirtatiously say, "No, you said you have to have me. You think I'm going to just jump into bed with you?"

"No, you could walk, crawl, skip—you don't have to jump—but I'll *have* you," he says, smiling confidently. "So, is there a time you think you can get away?"

I know there is, but should I tell him and set things in motion or listen to Mark and end this thing now? "My kids have their school exploratory trips in a couple of weeks. Joey will be in Santa Cruz and Lance in Yosemite for five days. Steve will be away that week for a couple of days on business in San Francisco." OK, that was probably really stupid, but now it's out there.

"I'll arrange everything; you just show up. OK?" I don't respond. "Cass, OK?" he asks again.

"OK, Dan."

Twenty-One

$\mathcal{A}$ few days later, Daniel texts me before class and tells me to park away from the studio. After class I'll leave as usual and he'll text me once the studio clears out. Then I should go back in using the back door. After class I walk toward my car and get a text that it's OK to come in. I walk in. He locks the door behind me and practically throws me against the wall and starts kissing me.

"Dan." I stop him. "First, I haven't showered. Second, this isn't safe."

He continues kissing me and says, "You smell amazing. You always smell amazing. No one is coming, Cass, not till later." I kiss him back as passionately as I want to. Daniel's shirt is off, and he starts working mine off. We never can seem to get close enough. We hear something at the front door. It sounds like someone's trying to open it.

Daniel says quietly, "Who the hell is that?" He quickly walks to the front desk, and I run into the women's dressing room.

"Hey, honey." This can't be happening! It's Cheryl! I look for an escape route that I already know doesn't exist. All I can do is pray she has no reason to come back here. I'm being as quiet as I can.

"Hi, Cheryl. This is a surprise!" *Gee, Daniel, that's the understatement of the year!*

"I just want to get some computer and paperwork done that I've been putting off," she replies.

"Hey, I'm hungry. Why don't we go grab a bite to eat first, and then you can come back and do what you need to do?" he asks her. *Good thinking, Dan, just get her out of here so I can make it to the nearest emergency room and have cardio electrical shock therapy to bring my heart rate down.*

"Yeah, that would be great. Let's go," she says happily. *Thank God*, I think!

I hear them walking out the front door when Daniel says, "Go on ahead, Cheryl. Let's take your car. I want to open a few windows and make sure all the heaters are off." I hear her leave, and he comes over to the women's changing room to give me the thumbs-up. I take off out the back door. He says he'll call or text later.

Crap that was close. That's what I always worry about, that one slip that'll bring everything to light.

⌒

That night I tell Steve I'm thinking about going to a yoga retreat for a couple of days while the kids are on their explorations and he's in San Francisco. "Cass, why don't you come with me to San Francisco? I'll be busy during the day, but at night we can go out for dinner and have some quality time together."

That throws me for a loop. He rarely asks me to go on his business trips with him. "No, Steve, I don't think so. I was kind of hoping to just escape for a few days while I have the opportunity. Besides, I'd be spending the days alone while you're in meetings. Maybe another time," I reply.

"OK, Cass, but let's plan a weekend together soon, just you and me," he says, putting his arms around my waist.

"Yeah, that would be great. We need that," I quietly respond, resting my head on his chest."

I am struggling with my feelings for Steve, and certainly having Daniel in the mix confuses me even more. Daniel makes me feel like I am free falling, while Steve is my soft place to land. The feelings are different, and I still can't seem to make out how or why. My cell phone rings. I pull away from Steve, walk over, and pick up my phone. It's Mark.

"Hey, Mark, what's up?" I ask, kind of rolling my eyes in Steve's direction, as if to say, "Sorry."

"He's engaged!" Mark yells into the phone.

"Who's engaged, Mark?"

"Greg. Greg! The bastard is engaged!" he shouts again.

"I'm on my way."

I explain the crisis to Steve and tell him I have to go. He replies, not realizing he's being insensitive, "Shouldn't he be over that guy by now?" I just ignore his comment and leave.

⌒

I get to Mark's, and he's a mess. I walk over to the half-empty bottle of Scotch and ask, "How much have you had, Mark?"

He's sitting on the couch, legs stretched out, clinging to a pillow and staring at the ceiling. "Not enough, obviously, because this pit I have in my stomach is still here."

I sit on the couch next to him. "So, when did he tell you?"

"Cass, he didn't tell me. I heard it from a mutual friend who was at the engagement celebration."

"Ouch, what a coward!" I exclaim. "Sorry, Mark, I truly am!"

He's still sitting the same way, staring at the ceiling. "He has the indecency to keep coming over here and sharing my bed but not the decency to at least let me know personally that he's getting engaged. I didn't even know he was in a committed relationship," he says with disbelief.

"Mark, 'decency,' 'committed,' and 'Greg' in the same sentence are oxymorons."

"Cass, I loved him. I really did. I still love him," he says emotionally.

"I think at first you did, Mark, but after you found out all the lying, cheating, and manipulating he was doing, you stayed in love with the idea of who you *thought* he was. You'd never fall in love with someone like that if that's who you thought he was from the beginning. That's what you've been clinging to, an idea of who you thought he was, nothing else. Think about it. If he introduced himself to you and said, 'Hi, my name is Greg. I'm going to first seduce your mind and heart, your body will follow, and after you've invested so much time in me emotionally and fall completely in love with me, I'll have already been lying and cheating on you, even with some of your friends. It won't matter though, and here's where it really gets good. You'll have been so busy being exactly who and what I want you to be that you'll completely lose any idea of the person you were before me. You won't even know where I end and you begin.'" I gently say, "Now, Mark, if he'd put it to you that way when you first met, would you have fallen in love with him?"

He laughs slightly as tears fill his eyes. "That's exactly what happened, isn't it? And no, of course I wouldn't have fallen for him."

"See, you're still the confident, incredible person that I know and love so much, but it's like you're caught in the spin cycle of a washing machine that won't turn off. You have the power to turn it off, to stop this vicious cycle, because even if he's engaged, you and I both know he's not done with you. Take who you are back. Let the idea go. Change your mind, Mark. Change your mind."

"I love you, sweet Cass. Will you share some Scotch with me?"

"Sure, just a little bit, but then I'm getting you to bed. I love you too, Mark."

*D*aniel sends me a text that all is set for the following week. He's found a log cabin in the mountains. He sends me pictures of the outside and inside. He knows I don't like roughing it, so I'm really pleased with what he's chosen. It's high end, with really elegant furniture. There's a stone fireplace that goes all the way up to the ceiling. The kitchen is modern with stainless-steel appliances and these really cool and interesting concrete counter tops. I love it, and I'm getting so excited. He did good again. He did good!

I text him, "Perfect!"

He replies, "It's going to be perfect, Cass."

My heart is aching for him. Next week can't come soon enough. I have everything picked out for our evening together. I bought some new lingerie—I chose a white, sheer silk babydoll with a matching thong. It took forever to pick something out, but I knew the second I put this on he'd love it.

*T*he weekend before we all set off for our trips, Steve and I decide to go out to dinner at our favorite Thai restaurant. When we get there, it's busy as usual. They don't take reservations, so they take our name and give us a beeper that will let us know when our table is ready. We decide to wait on the patio, and as we turn to walk out, I'm shocked to see Daniel and Cheryl walk in. I take a long inhalation and then exhale deeply. Daniel sees me and looks just as shocked as I am.

"Cassandra!" Cheryl says with excitement.

"Hi Cheryl, Daniel. How wonderful to see you guys! Steve, this is Cheryl and Daniel from yoga."

Steve extends his hand to shake theirs and says, "Nice to finally meet you. Cassandra speaks very highly of both of you. Hey, how about you join us for dinner?"

What? No! I scream in my head.

Daniel says, "Oh no, we wouldn't want to intrude."

At almost the same time, Cheryl says, "We'd love to!"

Steve says, "Great!" and goes up to the reception desk to tell them we're now four for dinner. Daniel and I look at each other with disbelief.

We're sitting on the patio making small talk when we're paged that our table is ready. We sit down, and Steve orders a bottle of their best sake. We all order appetizers. I'm sitting across from Cheryl and Steve across from Daniel. This couldn't feel more awkward.

Steve states, "So, Cass tells me you now have two studios. How's that going for you?"

Cheryl responds, "The studios are doing really well, but it's so much work, we hardly have time for much else. Our lives seem to be wrapped around the studios, which is fine. We really enjoy it, but I hope things will eventually settle once we get through these growing pains."

Steve comments, in his typical businesslike way, "Yes, I understand. It's very challenging starting a new business, even when you have an existing model that's working."

Daniel and I are silently drinking our sakes and exchanging quick glances like two deer caught in the headlights.

Daniel reaches for more sake, and I'm right behind him. Cheryl looks at Daniel and remarks, "You're drinking more than usual."

"Am I?" he asks.

Steve looks at me and, chuckling, says, "Yeah, so are you, Cass."

"Well, I love sake. You know, good company and good conversation make for better drinking," I reply, trying to sound relaxed.

"So, Cassandra," Cheryl asks, "how are the kids? I'm sorry, I forgot their names."

"Joey and Lance, or...L...for short...his nickname," Daniel answers. As he was talking, he realized he shouldn't have been. He began pausing between words and saying each word more quietly as he went along.

I look over at Steve. After so many years of marriage, you'd think I could read the look on his face, but I can't. There's a silence.

"Oh that's cute, L. Why L?" Cheryl asks me.

"Well, when Lance was a baby, Joey started calling him L, and it just stuck."

"That's sweet, isn't it, Daniel?" she says, looking over at him.

"Yes, very sweet," he says, half smiling.

"So, if I remember correctly, Joey is fifteen and Lance is twelve."

Steve corrects her and says, "No, Joey is just about to turn seventeen, and Lance is almost fifteen. They're going on their school trips next week for five days."

Daniel says, "They're really going to love Santa Cruz and Yosemite."

Smooth, Daniel, really smooth. Your wife barely knows the names and ages of my kids, and you know where they're going on their school trips.

"How about you guys? Do you have kids?" Steve asks.

"We have two, Brandon and Leah. Brandon is the musician of the family, and Leah is studying pre-med at the University of Michigan," Cheryl states proudly. She continues, "Brandon is just like his dad, same temperament, loves yoga, and loves his walkabouts."

Steve curiously asks, "Walkabouts? What's that exactly?"

She shares, "That's what Daniel does when he needs to get away from everything, you know, the studios, the city. It's an Australian term. He just takes off, goes hiking or walking, sometimes for days. He has this particular beach further north that he goes to. He's never even taken me there. That's his place to think, meditate, clear his mind."

Without thinking I say, "It's beautiful there." I look at Daniel, who looks like he's about to choke on his water. *What did I just say? Too much sake. How the hell do I backpedal out of this one? Here I go.* "At the beach, I mean. It's beautiful there, at the beach, anywhere. Aren't beaches beautiful, Steve?" *Good God above, what am I rambling about?*

"Yes," Steve says. "Every time we go on vacation, I want to go to London, France, Italy, somewhere cultural. Cass, you find her a beach in Hawaii, Tahiti, the Caribbean, anywhere really, and she's in heaven." Sweet, unsuspecting Steve saves me. That's my man! "Cass is going on a yoga retreat next week while the kids are on their trips and I'm in San Francisco. I think you said it was by the beach, didn't you, Cass?"

Just when I think things couldn't get any worse. *Think with the part of your brain that isn't saturated with sake, Cass. You get a single shot at this one.* I reply, "Well, there are two I'm considering. I haven't decided yet."

Cheryl asks, "Oh, which ones are those? Maybe I've heard about them."

Someone, anyone, change the subject, please. By the grace of something I've done somewhere right in my life, recent past excluded, the waiter comes up and asks if we're ready to order our entrées. "Yes," I reply a bit too quickly.

Daniel's right behind me. "Yes, yes we are."

Let's order, eat, and get out of here quickly because Daniel and I clearly do not have the skill set to deal with this type of situation.

We order, and then Cheryl says, "Oh, Daniel's going on one of his walkabouts this coming week, hiking up in Yosemite." Everyone is quiet now. Cheryl and Steve aren't saying anything.

I'm wondering—and I'm fairly certain Dan is as well—if they're quiet because they're doing the algebra in their heads and the variables are about to be found out. I'm convinced that blown-wide-open thing is about to happen. Steve finally says, "Maybe you'll run into Lance up there."

Cheryl laughs and replies, "Wouldn't that be funny?"

We all laugh. For the first time all evening, I breathe. I feel like I've been holding my breath for the last hour and a half. The waiter comes up and asks if we'd like coffee and dessert. At the same time, Daniel and I say, with the same amount of conviction, "No, thank you."

Steve says, "Just the check, please." Steve offers to take care of dinner, but Daniel won't hear of it. They split the bill, and we walk outside to say our good-byes.

"We should do this again sometime. We had a really wonderful time," Cheryl says sincerely.

"Yes, we should. It was a pleasure to finally meet you," Steve replies, shaking their hands.

Cheryl and I give each other a hug. "See you in class. Have fun at your retreat," she says kindly.

"Thanks, Cheryl. I will. Take care."

"Bye Cass—Cass…Cassandra," Daniel says, trying to recover, knowing very few people call me Cass. I'm hoping Steve just thinks he has a speech impediment.

"Bye, Daniel," I reply.

We get in our car, and Steve says, "They're really nice people, Cass. I see your attraction to that studio."

Attraction, yes, there's that. "Yeah, they are," I say, thanking the stars above that dinner is over. I never want to go through something like that again!

⌒

The following Monday, the kids are off on their trips. Joey is more excited than Lance. L, like me, prefers not to rough it. Camping isn't something he particularly enjoys. He loves the outdoors and hiking but would much prefer coming back to a nice hotel with showers and a comfortable bed afterward.

I ask Mark to come over that morning. I've been putting off telling him about my plans with Daniel this week, but I know if I tell him after the fact he'll be hurt and upset with me. I make coffee and get the bagels ready for his arrival. When Mark walks in, he looks like he hasn't been sleeping or eating much.

"Mark, you look exhausted, and a meal now and again might actually do you some good," I say, concerned.

"I'm doing the best I can, Cass. No lectures please," he replies curtly. He changes the subject. "So, what are we going to do this week with all this time you have on your hands? There's this great Argentinian band performing at the Attic. Want to go?"

"When will they be playing?" I reply, hoping it misses the evening Daniel and I will be together.

"Wednesday. We can grab a bite at that Mexican restaurant you like, then catch the show."

"I can't, Mark," I say as I pour him his coffee and finish toasting the bagels.

"Why, hot date?" I think he's joking but can't tell.

"Yeah, actually," I say quietly.

"Now, how did I know that?" he comments. I guess he was serious. "What and where? The *when* I now know; the *who* I know. It's the *why* I'm having a hard time with." He speaks very calmly.

"I know, Mark. We're going up to a log cabin in the mountains, just for one night," I passively respond.

"Well that explains the what and where. What about the why? What could possibly come out of this? Look, Cass, we've been around the block a few times. We both have been on the receiving end and the giving end of cheating, so it's not like this is unfamiliar territory for us. Having that knowledge, why do you want to put yourself and your family out there like that? What's the quote by Maya Angelou that you always tell your kids when they mess up? Oh yeah, 'When we know better, we do better,' right? You know better, so where is the doing better with this thing with Daniel? Can you answer that for me?" He's still quite calm, almost resigned to the fact that no matter what he says, this is going to happen.

"I don't know the why in a logical or rational way. I can't intellectualize this, not for myself and not for you. I'm going with pure emotion, which I know, intelligently speaking, considering my circumstances, isn't the wisest thing I could be doing," I say, trying to explain it the best way I know how.

"Cass, you're going to do exactly what your heart wants to do, regardless of what I say, but I wouldn't be the friend I am to you if I didn't speak my truth about the situation. No matter what you decide, I'm not going to love or respect you any less. Just know that, OK?" he says supportively.

Steve leaves on Tuesday night for San Francisco and is scheduled to be back late Thursday evening. Wednesday morning, I get ready for my evening with Daniel. We'll meet at the cabin at around six o'clock. We're taking separate cars. The drive is about two hours. He's going to stay an extra night and do some hiking, but I'm only comfortable with one night. I take a long, hot shower, using my favorite lavender soap and shampoo. I want everything to be perfect for this evening.

I get dressed, make some tea, and sit out on our back patio. It's a clear day, so I have a beautiful view of the ocean. I wonder what Daniel's doing. I can't stop thinking about him and can't wait to be in his arms again, tasting his kisses, feeling his body close to mine. This time there'll be absolutely no holding back. Three years of emotions and sexual tension finally realized. I'm aroused just thinking about it. I already miss his smell, his touch, the way he moans with desire when he rubs against me and kisses my neck.

I get a text from Daniel. "Leaving a little early. See you soon."

I answer, "Should be on the road in about an hour. Drive carefully."

"You too, Cass."

I get another text. This one from Mark. "Love you, Cass. See you tomorrow."

I reply, "Love you, Mark. See you then."

The drive up to the cabin seems much longer than two hours. The road is winding, filled with sharp turns. It makes me dizzy, and I can't wait to get there already. It's starting to get dark as I pull up to the cabin. I see Daniel's car, and my heart starts to race. My stomach feels like a butterfly pavilion. The cabin is absolutely beautiful from the outside, surrounded by trees, and it's much bigger than I expected. Daniel really went out of his way to find a nice place for us.

I sit in my car, trying to catch my breath for a few minutes. I finally open my car door but don't get out yet. The lights in the cabin are on, and I see Daniel step up to the front floor-to-ceiling window with what looks like a beer in one hand and the other hand on his hip. He must've heard me drive up and is wondering where I am. The interior lights are on in my car, and he can see me clearly. He stares at me, motionless, and I stare at him. I start to think about everything Mark said, especially how on the road in life, there are no U-turns; a road once traveled can't be untraveled. I think about Joey and Lance, even Cheryl and the way she spoke of her children, Brandon and Leah, with such pride and love. What about Steve and all the years between us? Daniel doesn't come out, and I'm still in my car—we're staring at each other.

In a split second, my mind is made up. I close my car door, put my car in reverse, and start to pull out. I look up for a second and see Daniel looking down at the floor. I finish pulling out and head back home. Mark's right; he has been all along. It's better for Daniel and me to hurt from letting this go than to allow the carnage that could follow from a decision like this. Daniel was also right; our feelings for each other aren't wrong. They aren't even right. They just are. Our circumstances may determine what we do with how we feel, right or wrong, but they're our circumstances, and no amount of denial is going to change that. The feelings we have—however real, powerful, beautiful, and strong—won't change them either. So, we can have our feelings—maybe we can't control that—but how we react and what we choose to do with them is entirely up to us. That we can control. I chose to walk toward them for a while, and now I choose to walk away, for all the right reasons.

It's like I was telling Mark—we don't always get it right. Sometimes we do; sometimes we don't. Life isn't a test; life is an exploration. No one will be handing out report cards at the end of this. All that really matters, when all is said and done, is our intention, how we loved those around us and how we were loved. That's all that's ours; everything else stays here.

I'm overwhelmed with emotions as I head back down that winding road. It feels just like the road I've been on for the past three years. I say out loud, "Thanks, Daniel, for giving me all those beautiful moments in time. Thanks for being my bungee jump and my skydive."

Without calling him, I drive straight to Mark's house. I'm so happy he's home. I knock on the door, and he answers.

"Cass!" he exclaims, happy and excited to see me. He can tell I've been crying and gives me a hug.

Then I hear someone say, "Hi, Cass. Long time no see." To my horror it's Greg. He's standing behind Mark.

"It's Cassandra, and not long enough, Greg," I say angrily.

Mark says very sternly, "Like I said before Cass got here, it's time for you to go, Greg, and never show up uninvited again." I look up at Mark and smile. *Wow, it's about time.* Greg starts to walk out, and Mark says, "Leave your key, Greg." Greg takes the key off his key chain, throws it on the coffee table, and walks out without saying a word.

"I'm so proud of you, Mark. That was amazing!"

"Yup," he says. "Time to stop existing and start living." I smile and give him big hug and start crying all over again. He walks me over to the couch and sits down.

I lie down with my head on his lap. "My heart hurts, Mark. It really hurts. I want to be with Daniel."

"It's going to be OK, Cass. It'll hurt for a while, but it'll be OK. Everything always works out. I'm proud of you too, Cass, really proud."

"He still had a key?" I ask, surprised.

"Did I forget to mention that to you?" he replies jokingly. "Spend the night here, OK, Cass? I'm going to make us some of my famous gin and tonics, and you make us sandwiches."

"You got it. I'm going to get my overnight bag from the car and call Steve to let him know I've had a change of plans."

"Sounds good, really good," he says with a big smile.

As I'm walking to my car, I get a text from Daniel. There's no message, just a link to a song with lyrics. It's Journey's "Separate Ways (Worlds Apart)." I plug my phone into my car stereo, click on the link, and listen to it.

I cry through the entire song. I miss him so much and want to be with him right now. Part of me wishes I'd stayed, but the other part knows this is what's right and the only possible outcome of an impossible situation.

Mark taps on the window. "Cass, sweetie, you OK?" He opens my door, sees I'm in tears, and takes me inside. He hands me my drink and says, "Doing the right thing isn't always easy, but it's always the right thing. Hang in there, Cass, and I'll hang in there with you."

"You too," I respond. "What you did with Greg—that took some serious courage, and I'm right here with you."

We raise our glasses, and Mark makes a toast. "To true friendship, which knows no above and beyond, only here, now, and always."

"Cheers to that, Mark!"

Twenty-Two

It's been over a month since I've seen Daniel. Neither one of us has texted or called the other. I made a decision, and that's the end of it. Life is back to details and routines. I think sometimes I should take up a hobby, something to help get my mind off of Daniel. It seems like everything reminds me of him. Around the house Steve knows something's up. I'm very quiet and subdued; having a conversation with me is an exercise in futility. I don't have much to say. The worst part is I'm doing with my kids what I've always been very critical with Steve about. I'm physically there but not present mentally. They can ask me a question three or four times before I realize I'm being spoken to. I've explained that I'm distracted and just missing my brother and dad. I apologize and ask for their patience.

I've changed studios, and while I still love the yoga, I'm feeling less inspired and miss practicing and taking classes from Dan. Mark's going through similar feelings about Greg and keeps telling me time will heal this ache we're feeling, but I'm not so sure. I listen to that Journey song constantly. My family is sick of it, but I can't hear it enough. I've driven to "our" beach and taken long walks along the shoreline, retracing our footprints and reliving the memories. I sit and stare at the ocean, wishing for some epiphany to hit me that will make sense of all of this, hoping for some insight that will magically fill this void, this emptiness, and take away the longing I feel for him.

I found a perfect sand dollar on one of my trips there, and I keep it on my nightstand. I look at it when I'm trying to fall sleep, remembering the story Daniel told me and the intimate moments that followed. I still don't feel regret; I think I'm supposed to. I guess there are a lot of supposed-to-bes and should-bes in life, but what purpose do they serve in the current moment? I don't even regret driving away that evening from the cabin. Do I think about what that night might have been like? Do I think about every brilliant moment Daniel and I shared? Do I think about the talks, the laughter, the desire, the want between us? Only all the time, but I have no regrets.

⟨⟩

One Saturday I ask Steve to come with the kids and me to the mountains for the day. I'll pack a lunch, and we can hike and just hang out. He says he's too busy and for us to go and have a good time. I call Mark to see if he wants to go. "Hey, Mark, I know it's last minute, but I was going to make a picnic lunch and head up to the mountains with the kids. Care to join us?"

"I'd love to. I'll be right over," he says enthusiastically.

"Yay, see you soon!" I happily reply.

Mark arrives and I have everything ready. Lance brings a football and Frisbee, and Joey is complaining that her hiking shoes aren't flattering and what if she runs into someone she knows.

"Joey, we'll be hiking, therefore the hiking shoes. And in the unlikely event that you run into one of your friends hiking, they'll probably be wearing hiking shoes as well, so it's a wash." She rolls her eyes and makes this ugh sound, like I'm so clueless to the ways of the new generation.

We start our drive. The kids are in the back; they have their earphones on listening to music, so they can't hear our conversation. Mark quietly says, "Look, it's OK, but we're going to that spot you and Daniel used to go to, aren't we?" My best friend knows me so well.

"Yes. It's strange, Mark, but by going to the places we used to go I feel close to him somehow."

"Cass, I do the same thing. I wish I started this getting-over-Greg thing two years ago. Maybe I'd be over him by now."

I respond, sounding defeated, "That's not reassuring. I have how many years of this left to go? Mark, it's not getting easier; if anything, it's getting harder. I think if it ended badly, like with a fight or even with its blowing up in our faces with Steve and Cheryl finding out, I could get past this quicker. I can't get him out of my head—no, my heart—both, my head and my heart." I'm irritated as I try to explain myself.

"Cass, stop judging it. Just go with it. Feel the pain. Embrace it. You do that with Andy and your dad, and you work through it. You'll never get over that loss, but when a wave hits hard you hang on and ride it out. Maybe you—we—could approach this the same way."

I ask Mark sincerely, "Do you miss your mom the same way you miss Greg? Do you hurt the same way? Is that emptiness and longing to see and feel her the same?"

Mark takes a long inhalation and says very simply, "No, not even close."

I look over at him for a second. "I know, Mark. It's different. Although it looks like it should be the same, the loss, the sadness, the heartache, the void—it couldn't be more different. I think because death demands an end, there's nothing left but memories. There's a hopelessness and a finality that comes with death. Everyone talks about closure. Death is closure. But while we're living there's no closure. There's acceptance, evolution, growth, transformation, but no closure. With this, no matter how hard we try to push it aside, there's hope, hope for what might have been and might still be. We fight it, but there it is, every second of every day. Hoping we'll run into them, hoping things can be different, hoping we can have what we once had, hoping for just one more moment with them, and even hoping that we can forget them.

"Death of someone you love destroys hope. None of that's possible, so you resign yourself to that fact, and acceptance and surrender are the only alternative. This—what we're going through—is like living in purgatory. Acceptance one way or the other is unacceptable. We'll get through it—of course we will— but how and what will it look like on the other side of this, who we'll be, how we'll be? That we can't know yet."

Mark sighs, "Hell, Cass, you sure are a downer!" I laugh. He adds, "Everything you said is true, so very true. I wish it wasn't, but it is."

I put my hand on his thigh and tell him it'll be OK, maybe not as soon as we'd like it to be, but we'll get there.

We get to the picnic grounds, and as I step out of the car I'm immediately emotional. I walk over to Mark and put my arm around his waist. He puts his arm around my shoulder. We stand there and try and take in the beauty of the scene in front of us. Something is missing though; something feels off. We both sense it.

Mark shouts to Lance, "Hey, where's the football?"

Lance holds it up. "Right here, Mark. Go long!" he exclaims.

Mark runs as Lance throws him the football. "Perfect spiral, Lance. That's the way to do it. You're the man!" My kids love Mark almost as much as I do.

Joey is texting. I think her hands are permanently attached to her phone. "Joey, come on. Put your phone away and enjoy this time with us."

She looks up exasperated. "In a minute, Mom."

I walk over to the big boulder where Daniel and I did Standing Bow Pose, the Cosmic Dancer. I climb up and start doing the pose. *Breathe, Cass,* I say to myself. *Breathe into that place inside of you that's so expansive and fill it with the love and joy that's you...and Daniel.* Mark climbs up and gets into Bow with me. We hold the pose for a very, very long time. We release and do the other side, slowly moving into the posture, gracefully and with the full integrity this posture deserves and demands.

Here we are, Cosmic Dancers, on this road called life, breathing, surrendering, detaching, releasing, and accepting the choices and decisions we've made. We come out of the pose and are standing high on this boulder, our eyes closed, hands by our sides, palms facing forward. We both inhale deeply all the energy around us and try to exhale all that no longer serves us. We'll learn to let go. We'll grow, and we'll transform. It'll just take patience, time, and acceptance.

Twenty-Three

I lie on my couch listening to—what else?—Journey's "Separate Ways (Worlds Apart)." I have it on a loop on my iPad. I always believed in the saying that time heals all wounds. That was before I lost two of the most influential men in my life. I'm realizing time is just time; it carries no magic with it. The wound of losing my father and brother back to back is still there, not scarred over or healed. That doesn't mean I'm not healed in many other ways; their deaths have healed many wounds from my past and opened my heart in ways I could've never imagined. The loss will always be there, and that's OK. I've made my peace with that. The loss of Daniel—that's still open and raw, and I'm waiting on time to heal that wound. I'm not holding my breath, though. I wonder if it's the same for him.

Steve comes in and lowers my music. I give him a disappointed look. "Cass, I know what this is. I know why you listen to this song all the time and why you're so distant and quiet lately. It's not only your dad and Andy; it's more than that. It's been eating me up on the inside."

How could he possibly know? I wonder. It's been a few months since I've seen Daniel; there are no texts or voice messages to be found. The only way he could know is if Mark told him, and Mark would never do that to me. Strange, though. I'm not worried at all. My heart isn't racing. I'm not thinking of a story or a justification I could tell him. I'm resigned to the fact that, however he found out, it's for the better, so let's just get this over with. Whatever the consequences, I'm ready to face them.

He looks down and says very quietly, "Jennifer and I—we did sleep together, one time, a long time ago. It was only once, and during that time you and I were practically strangers. You were so angry all the time and so defensive—"

I interrupt and reply, indifferently, "So, your sleeping with Jennifer is my fault? My anger's fault? My defenses' fault? Where do you come into play? Where is your responsibility in all of this?" I'm not surprised. I always knew in my heart they'd crossed boundaries.

"I'm sorry, Cass. I'm not saying it was your fault. I'm just trying to take you back to that time and all we were going through, and it only happened that one time."

I reply dryly, "Steve, this only-one-time thing is a cop out. If it was some stranger you met at a bar and you ended up having a one-night stand and never saw her again, that's a one-time thing. You and Jennifer—no, that wasn't one time. You're ignoring all that happened leading up to your sleeping with her. That's harder for me to swallow than the actual act itself. It probably started with a look that lasted longer than usual or a touch that lingered a bit too long. Then a lunch or two here and there. From there it could have progressed to drinks and dinners; you shared your feelings and part of yourself with her. There was an underlying sexual tension that ultimately culminated in you two sleeping together. Am I warm, Steve? Isn't that the way it happened?"

He nods his head in agreement.

"You see, it wasn't just once. Everything that happened leading up to that was as out of line as the act itself," I say, sounding like someone who knows exactly what I'm talking about from experience. "You slept with Jennifer a long time ago, and she's still working for you? That's interesting, Steve, really interesting,"

He weakly replies, "We've been able to compartmentalize things, Cass. It's just business now and has been for a long time."

Here I am white-knuckling it, trying to get over Daniel, while Steve and Jennifer are putting their feelings in compartments. How sweet! "Compartmentalize things? Is that something you have to work on, or are you both naturally gifted that way? Has it ever occurred to you to fire her and get rid of the temptation after what you two shared?"

"I've considered it, but since nothing has happened since and she's also married with children to support I couldn't do that."

Is he purposely trying to get under my skin? I can't believe what he said, and I'm trying to remain calm because I don't have the energy to argue. "How incredibly noble of you. I've met very few altruistic people—maybe none—and here I am, all these years, living with one right under my nose."

"If you want me to fire her, I will, Cassandra. Whatever it takes to save our marriage, I'll do it. I love you, Cass."

"That's assuming way too much, Steve. You're assuming that, after this revelation, there's a marriage to be saved. Fire her. Don't fire her. I don't care what you do." I'm sitting up now, hands on my face. I can't look at him. I can't cry. I can't think. I can't even hurt. I understand what he's saying. I remember that time; it was awful. We *were* like strangers. I was distant, and he was working constantly—though he was obviously doing more than working some nights. Who am I to judge what he did, considering what I did? Daniel and I never slept together, but we may as well have. What Daniel and I had went beyond a physical attraction; it was emotional. We shared our thoughts, our feelings, our minds, our souls, and to some extent our bodies.

I love Steve, and I miss Steve, which is why I've had such a hard time figuring this thing out with Daniel. Are they different kinds of love? Does one transcend the other? Is one more honest than the other? Are they equal but separate? I don't know. If I did I wouldn't be sitting on this couch listening to that song on a constant loop, making even my cats run for cover. I start crying, not only because of what Steve told me, but mostly for Daniel and how much I miss him. I can't even describe the loneliness I feel without him in my life. I don't look forward to my days like I used to. I wear the necklace and bracelet he gave me all the time. I'm forever reliving the moments we shared, the way he laughs, the way he smiles, his boyish charm and grin, his passion, his enthusiasm and love for life, his yoga, his kisses, and his scent.

I start crying harder, and Steve tries to hold me. I push him away and shout, "Don't you dare touch me, not now and maybe not ever! Do not touch me!" I'm aware of the double standard I have going, but I am too hurt to really care about it.

He pleads, "Cass, please. We can work this out, get counseling, whatever it takes."

"Leave me alone. I don't want to talk about this. Leave me alone. Just leave!" I yell. After all these years together, he knows better than to force any issue when I'm like this, and he walks out of the room. I'm in mourning, and I don't want Steve and his attack of conscience encroaching upon that sacred space. I want to be left alone to mourn the loss of Daniel in peace. His intrusion isn't welcome or wanted. I find myself resenting that more than his sleeping with Jennifer.

Twenty-Four

ife with Steve, since he confessed about his relationship with Jennifer, has gone from bad to worse. We make every effort around the kids to keep things civil. He's replaced Jennifer and found her a job with one of his investors. "How considerate and thoughtful of you to go out of your way for her like that," I commented sarcastically to him when he told me. I believe he was trying to be thoughtful and considerate of me, but it's only been a month since I found out about them so any leeway I could give him, I won't.

He sleeps in the guest room. We've sat the kids down and explained that so much has happened in these past years, we're trying to figure things out. "Are you guys getting a divorce?" they always ask.

I'm honest and tell them, "We're not sure where this will end up, but our love for you is eternal, and your dad and I will always love each other as well, but it may become a different kind of love. We just don't know yet."

Mark's very sad as well. He likes Steve, and he likes Steve and me together. I like Steve and me together. When he's present and engaged with the kids and me, he's a joy to be around. He's funny, kind, loving, and supportive. It's just that as wonderful as those moments are, his business dominates, so those times aren't as often as they could be. I thought of calling Daniel after this all happened, just like I thought about calling him after that time Steve took Jennifer's call in the middle of our argument. I can't do that. I don't ever want this thing with Daniel to be about Steve and me, or like I'm out for some kind of revenge. That's not fair to Daniel nor to Steve. I need to manage and figure out my feelings for Dan and try to understand how to move forward with my life, with or without Steve. There's too much at stake to act impulsively or reactively. One would think the passage of time would've somehow eased my feelings for Daniel, but no, not even close. I still miss him and think of him with the same intensity as I did driving away from the cabin.

I head to the six p.m. Tuesday class at the new studio I've been going to. It's not where I want to be practicing, but it's a necessary adjustment I've made. As I'm driving, I think about how Daniel teaches at six-thirty tonight, but I try to not let my mind wander there. *Willpower, Cass,* I keep telling myself, *willpower.* I'm feeling particularly down tonight, though, so fighting this urge is more difficult than usual. I compare it to that day on the beach when I turned and walked away from Dan then found myself running back toward him. I keep telling myself, *Drive to your destination, no detours, Cass. You can do it.* This pep talk isn't working. I need a sponsor, someone completely objective, like they have in AA, to help me from falling off the wagon. Even Mark isn't strong enough to help me fight this feeling I have inside and talk me off this ledge.

I turn around. That's it. I'm going to Daniel's six-thirty class. On the way there I wonder if I'm going to be hit with an iceberg but decide to take my chances anyway. I park my car and start, once again, to talk myself out of it. So much time has passed I shouldn't even consider dipping my toes back into that water. I grab my stuff and make my way to the front door, pause, take a deep breath, and walk in. Dan looks up and sees me. The look on his face surprises me. He has a slight smile and such love and warmth in his eyes—not what I was expecting at all. He walks over to me, and in front of quite a few people, gives me a warm embrace and whispers how happy he is to see me. I hold him close and breathe in his scent. I whisper in his ear, "I miss you, Daniel. I miss you so much." He holds me a little tighter, then lets go.

I sign in, walk into the yoga room, and place my mat down in my favorite corner. I'm on the verge of tears at such a kind and loving reception. It's a busy class tonight. As class begins, I notice Daniel has left half the lights off, making the class dimmer, not bright like usual. He's his normal, confident, beautiful self. He guides us mindfully and thoughtfully into each pose. I've missed him so much, all of him. The way he teaches is inspired, and I'm happy to be in my corner, on my mat, in his class.

Triangle Pose is next, and while we're in the first set he tells us we're going to hold the second set longer than usual. We begin the second set. He gets us into the pose and then comes up right behind me. Giving instruction to the whole class, he says, "Really stretch your left hand up toward the ceiling while simultaneously stretching your right hand down toward your big and second toes." He's stretching my hand up as he gives the instruction, then glides it down to my left shoulder. His right hand is on the inside of my right thigh. He leans into me and whispers in my ear, "I've made love to you a million times in my mind…"

He speaks to the class again, "Now use your right elbow to press your knee back even more, bringing both of your knees in line. He comes back to me and whispers again, "But I don't ever have to make love to you…" He gives more instruction to the class. "Bring your left shoulder back and your right shoulder forward, bringing both your shoulders in line." He leans in again and softly says, "…to know how much I love you…" Back speaking to the entire class he says, "Strengthen and lengthen your left leg. Push into the outer edge of your left foot. Twist your upper body back. Reach and stretch."

I'm so relieved this is a hot yoga class so no one can tell my tears from my sweat. I'm sure Daniel can, though. It feels like the entire front of his body is now pressing into my back. I can feel his breath on my neck as he whispers once again in my ear, "I'm in with love you, Cass. I'll always love you." He slowly moves away from me and says authoritatively, "Change, other side..."

The End?

About the Author

Nina C. Payne is a wife, a mother of two, and a yoga instructor. Her love of yoga goes beyond physical postures, and she finds great pleasure in studying the philosophy, psychology, and physiology of yoga. Her debut novel, *Moments in Time,* is strongly inspired by her real-life experiences. Having lost her brother to cancer and then her father four months later to a broken heart, it explores the obstacles many of us face and the courage it takes to overcome them. She is also a poet with a passion for reading, music, hiking, rain forests, cooking, and long walks on the beach.